A NOTE TO READERS

Although the Flemings and their friends are fictional, the situations they find themselves in are real. The crash at the beginning of the story actually happened. A prototype of the B-29 crashed during a test flight, causing power outages in south Seattle and killing nineteen workers in a meatpacking plant. Because the B-29 was still top secret, the newspapers did not report the full story at the time.

Collecting paper, metal, and fat was an ongoing part of the war effort. Learning to live without as many sweets was also. After two years of war, families were becoming used to the shortages and found other ways to celebrate special events.

Some people in the United States were arrested for spying during the war, and schoolchildren were encouraged to be careful about what they said to others. "Loose lips sink ships" was one of the most famous mottoes of the war. While they weren't actually on the front lines, American citizens felt very much a part of the effort to win World War II.

SISTERS IN TIME

Jennie's War

THE HOME FRONT IN WORLD WAR 2

BONNIE HINMAN

BARBOUR
PUBLISHING

Jennie's

War

*For my dad, Floyd Wirts, a World War II veteran,
and for my uncles, Hank, Bob, Joe, Ray, Calvin, Wendell, Ole, and Bill,
who all served with distinction at home or abroad during the war.*

Cover design by Lookout Design Group, Inc.

Published by Barbour Publishing, Inc., P.O. Box 719, Uhrichsville, Ohio 44683
www.barbourbooks.com

*Our mission is to publish and distribute inspirational products offering exceptional value
and biblical encouragement to the masses.*

Member of the
Evangelical Christian
Publishers Association

Printed in the United States of America.

CONTENTS

1. The Mysterious Fire 9
2. Mr. Romano's Cousin 18
3. Sliding into Trouble 27
4. The Secret Weapon 36
5. Manure Tea 48
6. The Victory Garden Contest 57
7. Goats and Floats 67
8. Birthday Surprises 81
9. The Junk Car 92
10. More Clues 101
11. The Spy's Lair 113
12. Time Runs Out 122
13. Winners 132

CHAPTER 1

The Mysterious Fire

Jennie Fleming struggled with an old tire that was almost as big as she was.

"You can't take that on the bus," Tommy said to his older sister.

"Oh yes I can," Jennie said, puffing from the hard work. "This tire is going in my pile of scrap. I found it behind that building, and it's mine." She stopped and pulled her woolen cap down farther over her curly, dark hair.

Tommy shrugged and adjusted the basket he carried. It was full of old bicycle tubes and tires and a couple of worn-out rubber boots. They each had a pile of scrap rubber in the alley behind the hotel where they lived. They would divide this basketful between the piles, but they couldn't divide the big tire. It was only a few days before the end of the scrap rubber drive, and each wanted to have the most rubber to turn in at the collection center.

"At least hurry up," Tommy said. "Art and Jasper will be waiting for us."

Arthur—better known as Art—was their older brother. He and his friend Jasper had let Jennie and Tommy tag along for once. It was a school holiday, but the older boys were working on a school project. Nine-year-old Jennie and eight-year-old Tommy had begged to be included until Arthur gave in and said they could come along to look for scrap in a new neighborhood.

"Tommy, don't boss me. Remember, I'm older than you," Jennie said.

"Only by a year," Tommy said.

"I'm still older, and that makes you the baby of the family. Anyway, Art and Jasper won't be back at the bus stop yet," Jennie said. "They said to be back in an hour, and it hasn't been that long yet because I heard a noon whistle from one of the factories farther south not fifteen minutes ago."

Tommy switched the basket to his other hand. "I think all the rubber we have at home is enough to make an airplane tire."

"No, airplane tires are a lot bigger." Jennie tugged the tire over a curb.

"Not all of them," Tommy said. "There are little ones, too."

"How would you know? You've never been close to an airplane."

"Have so!" Tommy hollered over his shoulder.

"Have not!"

At first Jennie didn't pay any attention to the roar that grew steadily louder, but in seconds the air vibrated with sound. She only had time to look at Tommy and see a puzzled look on his face before a huge explosion knocked them off their feet. Their rubber scattered into the street.

Jennie lay on the sidewalk for a second or two, waiting and listening, but nothing else happened. She sat up and looked around, still clutching the big tire. "Tommy, are you all right?" Her brother sat nearby.

"I'm fine. What on earth was that?"

"I don't know. Some kind of explosion." Jennie jumped to her feet. People poured out onto the sidewalks and street. Everyone looked around and talked excitedly to each other.

"Look," Jennie said, "over there." She pointed south at a billow of smoke drifting above the rooftops of Seattle. Something was on fire, and by the looks of the smoke, it was something big. The wail of sirens in the distance soon cut through the babble of talk around the two.

"It was a plane! I saw it!" a woman yelled as she ran past them toward the smoke.

Jennie and Tommy looked at each other. Without a word, Jennie knew what her brother was thinking. Together they shoved Jennie's tire and the basket under a bush at the edge of the street and ran with everyone else toward the smoke. The need to meet Art and Jasper had vanished from their minds.

The fire was farther away than Jennie expected. The smoke had quickly stained the blue sky overhead gray and filled the air with a nasty smell. The closer they got to the main plume of smoke, the more people crowded the sidewalks. Some stared at the sky, but others hurried along with Jennie and Tommy toward the smoke's source.

At last they rounded a street corner and saw a fiery scene. Tall tongues of flame licked at a large building that sat back a little from the street. The fire's heat blew at them, along with smoke and cinders. Off to one side an electrical line dangled from a broken pole. It danced through the air like it was alive, shooting sparks in every direction. Jennie pulled at Tommy's arm to stop him. Maybe they were close enough.

"What was in that building?" Jennie yelled. A fire engine rounded the corner and sped past them, its siren screaming.

"A packing plant, where they cut up meat," a bystander said.

"There were probably people in there working," Jennie said. She swallowed hard. "Do you think they were killed?"

Tommy stared at the blazing building. "Maybe," he said slowly.

Moments later a woman ran past them. "Raymond! Raymond! Where are you?" the woman screamed. In a few moments she was out of sight, running toward the fire.

Jennie and Tommy stared at each other and then back at the fire. Police cars screeched to a halt in the street followed by military cars. More fire trucks arrived and ambulances followed. It was exciting in a horrible way, and Jennie and Tommy backed up a little and climbed on an old bench so they could watch.

A few minutes later the police moved everyone away from the fire. Jennie and Tommy escaped notice for a few minutes, but soon a policeman hollered at them to get down off the bench and move along. They obeyed, but Jennie stopped for one last look at the flames.

In the reddish-orange glow of the fire, she saw something that she hadn't noticed before. The flames had partly burned up the building, revealing the blackened skeleton of what looked like an airplane. She frowned and rubbed her eyes.

"Tommy, look at that." Jennie pointed at the building. "There—inside. It's an airplane. . .or what's left of one. But how did an airplane get in that building?"

Tommy stared for a moment and then raised his eyebrows. "It is a plane. Maybe it crashed."

"Remember that roaring noise right before the explosion? Maybe it was that airplane about to crash," Jennie said. "That's what the first woman was yelling."

"I told you kids to move along, didn't I?" The policeman had returned and gave them a ferocious look.

"We're going," Jennie said. "Did that plane crash into the building and start the fire?" She pointed at the plane framework, which was even more visible in the fire now.

The policeman didn't even look. "There's no plane. It was an explosion of some kind. Maybe gas. No plane involved. Now get a move on. This is a restricted area."

"But I can see the plane shape in the fire," Jennie persisted. "Just look."

"I said there is no airplane," the policeman snapped. "If you two don't hightail it out of here, I'm going to run you in."

At that, Jennie and Tommy took off down the sidewalk. In her haste, Jennie didn't see a man who was standing partly in the shadow of a nearby church. She ran right into the large, dark-haired man. The man muttered some words in a foreign language and brushed off Jennie as if she were a fly.

"I'm sorry, sir," Jennie said. "I wasn't looking." The man seemed not to hear and continued to stare toward the fire.

The pair ran for a couple of blocks before slowing and stopping by the side of a building.

"Tommy, I know I saw an airplane in that fire," Jennie said.

"I saw it, too. Why did the policeman say the opposite?"

"I don't know," Jennie replied. "It doesn't make sense. Let's go find Art and Jasper."

There was a lot in Jennie's life that didn't make sense these days. The war dragged on. She could barely remember what life was like before Japanese bombs had dropped out of the sky on Pearl Harbor more than two years ago. Her oldest brother, Roger, had enlisted in the army and was now serving in Europe. Jennie had never told anyone, but sometimes she couldn't remember what Roger looked like. When that happened, she stared at his picture on the living room table.

The older boys were waiting at the bus stop when Tommy and Jennie arrived.

"Where have you been?" Art said impatiently. "You two wouldn't notice if the street blew up under you if it meant getting some scrap for your collection."

"Wait until you hear what we saw," Jennie said, ignoring her brother's tone.

"Save it," Art ordered. He jerked his head at the oncoming bus. "Jasper and I were supposed to be back at the hotel by one o'clock to meet the coal delivery truck. You can explain to Mama why we're late." Jasper lived in the hotel, too, and he and Art both worked there after school and on Saturdays.

Everyone on the bus talked loudly about what they had seen, including the bus driver, who claimed to have snapped some pictures of a mysterious airplane flying low a few moments before the explosion. Not everyone agreed that it was an airplane, but they all had felt the jolt.

"Do you think they heard the explosion at home?" Jennie asked as they swung off the bus at the corner near the hotel.

"Maybe," Tommy said, "but I don't know how loud it would have been this far away."

"We'll find out in a minute." Jennie turned into the doorway and bounded up the stairs that led to the lobby of the hotel. Their family was running the hotel for some Japanese friends, the Tanakas, who had been sent to an internment camp soon after the war began. Art and Jasper ran for the back stairs to see if the coal delivery truck had come yet.

"It's so dark in here. Why aren't the lights on?" Jennie walked over to a wall switch and flipped it, but nothing happened. The only light shone dimly through the windows at the front of the lobby.

Their mother rushed out of the hotel office door. "There you are! I've been worried sick. What with the explosion and no electricity, I was thinking awful thoughts." She pulled the pair close for a hug. "Is Arthur with you?"

Jennie nodded and pointed toward the back of the building.

"Why on earth didn't you come home right away after that explosion? And don't tell me you didn't hear it. Everybody for miles around heard it."

Jennie looked at Tommy. She knew what he was thinking. How much should they tell? They would never lie to their mother, but some things were best left unsaid. Tommy raised his eyebrows and gave a tiny shoulder shrug. Jennie figured that meant Tommy thought they should tell the whole truth because Mama would find out anyhow.

"We were there," Jennie said finally.

"What do you mean?" Mama asked. She sounded suspicious. "I thought you were collecting rubber in the neighborhood."

"Oh, we were collecting rubber," Jennie said. "Just not in the neighborhood. Art and Jasper took us with them. We were right near the explosion, and an airplane was in the fire."

"But the policeman said it wasn't an airplane," Tommy said.

"Only it was," Jennie said, "because we both saw the shape of it in the fire. We think a plane crashed into that building and caused the fire. But we don't know why the policeman said it wasn't a plane."

Mama looked in stunned silence from one sibling to the other. "You mean to tell me that you went out of our neighborhood without telling me and then saw this fire or plane crash or whatever it was?" she said at last. She stood in the middle of the lobby with her arms crossed, frowning at her two youngest children.

"We didn't see the crash," Jennie said. "We heard it. It was afterward that we saw the fire and the plane." She avoided the first part of her mother's question.

"Don't tell me another thing right now." Mama raised her hands. "I don't want to know. You children will be the death of me yet. For now, get busy and find some extra candles. We don't know how long the power will be off, and our hotel guests will be needing light." She strode back to the office.

Jennie sneaked a grin at Tommy. Off easy so far. Maybe Mama would get busy and forget the whole thing. They started down the hall toward their apartment.

Mama stuck her head out of the office. "By the way, you haven't heard the last of this episode."

Jennie and Tommy groaned at the same time.

In a few minutes they were in the depths of a storage closet looking for candles.

"I was sure I saw some candles in here somewhere. You feel in the boxes on one side, and I'll do the other." Jennie shoved the closet door wide open to get every bit of light from the hallway. "I don't much like putting my hands into places I can't see first," she said.

"We're in enough trouble anyway, so we'd better just do it," Tommy said. "I guess it wasn't such a great idea to go with Art and Jasper today."

16

"It was a good idea," Jennie insisted, "but the wrong time." She felt among the boxes and other things stored on shelves.

"I'll say."

"Hey, I forgot," Jennie said. "We didn't stop and get our rubber and my tire."

"Forget about that stuff. We can get more," Tommy said.

Jennie knocked a box off the shelf, but there was no sound of breaking so she felt for it on the floor and shoved it back on the shelf.

"Of course you'd say that," Jennie muttered, "since it was my tire we left behind. Well, I'm not forgetting. Tomorrow I'm going after it."

"We probably won't be let out of the apartment for a month," Tommy said. "We'll probably be given bed detail."

"Yuck! I hope not, because I hate changing sheets." Jennie fumbled in yet one more box. "Here it is!" she yelled. The pieces of candle felt smooth to the touch. The small box was half full of assorted old and new candles. She tucked it under her arm and walked into the hallway with Tommy close behind.

Maybe Mama would be so happy to have the candles that she'd go easy on the two for leaving the neighborhood. It was more likely that Jennie would be changing dirty sheets, and the hotel never ran out of that item.

CHAPTER 2

Mr. Romano's Cousin

"When I was in the grocery store, a man said that it was a Japanese airplane trying to bomb the Boeing factory but it missed," Tommy said. He tossed dirty sheets on the pile in the hallway the Saturday after the crash.

Jennie shoved some of the sheets into a basket. "Dad has always said that Japanese planes couldn't come this far." She remembered the early days of the war when everyone was terrified that Japanese airplanes would swoop out of the sky just like they did at Pearl Harbor in Hawaii. Dad and Mama made sure that the hotel met all blackout restrictions in case of attack, but Dad still said that the Japanese couldn't fly the big bombers nearly this far. Dad was an engineer, so Jennie thought he should know.

"I heard a clerk say that an enemy agent blew up the meat-packing plant. He sure wasn't a very smart agent if that's what he thought was most important to blow up. Why wouldn't he blow up the shipyards or Boeing?" Tommy asked.

"Don't talk about blowing up Boeing. Dad says he is as safe as he can be working there," Jennie said.

"Maybe he just doesn't want us to worry," Tommy said.

Jennie frowned at her brother and jammed more dirty sheets in the basket. She handled a lot of her worries by keeping busy and thinking about other things, but it was hard to ignore the fact that her father worked in an important airplane factory. It made sense that the enemy would want to get rid of a factory that helped the United States so much.

"It was an airplane crash, not a bomb," Jennie said firmly. "We saw that with our own eyes. And I don't think it was a Japanese plane, either." She was having a hard time forgetting that fiery scene from the other day. She kept thinking about the woman who had called out for someone named Raymond. Maybe Raymond had died and left his wife and children to take care of themselves.

Jennie knew one thing for sure about war. It meant death—and plenty of it. She couldn't walk a block from her home in the hotel without seeing a gold star in a window showing that a soldier from that family had been killed. Somehow the disaster she had seen last week seemed worse, maybe because it was so close to home. Each night right after she prayed for Roger, she prayed for the families of the people who had died in the fire. She hoped God was listening.

"It must have been one of our planes," Tommy said after he tossed some wet towels into another basket. "But why would the government make such a secret of it? Planes have crashed around here before, and everyone knew."

"I don't know," Jennie said, "but I'm going to ask Dad about it again." The mystery of the plane in the fire was a puzzle she'd like to solve.

"He won't tell you anything." Tommy pushed the heavy basket down the hall.

Jennie sighed and picked up her overflowing basket. She knew Tommy was right. Dad probably wouldn't tell anything he might know about the crash. He was always quoting the war poster that said LOOSE LIPS SINK SHIPS. Dad said keeping quiet about war production, especially airplanes, was a serious matter. Jennie understood, but that didn't keep her from being curious. Maybe her best friend, Colleen Kramer, had heard something. They could talk after the Girl Scout meeting that afternoon while they hauled their crushed tin cans to the collection center. If she weren't on double duty here at the hotel because of their rubber-collecting expedition, Jennie would already be out with Colleen going door-to-door asking for tin cans. This hotel work never ended.

"Are we done yet?" Tommy asked after the last basket of dirty sheets and towels had been piled in the laundry room.

"No, and I want to get everything done before my Girl Scout meeting."

"Get the buckets then. All we have left is scrubbing the hall floor," Tommy said.

Jennie ducked back into the laundry room, muttering as she went. Tommy followed her and grabbed the mops off the rack where they hung. They were small mops, or Jennie and Tommy couldn't have managed them at all. In a few minutes they had partly filled two buckets with cleaner and water from the faucet over the laundry room sink.

Jennie set down her bucket in the hallway and stared at the faded linoleum floor. "How does this get so dirty?" There were muddy footprints down one side of the hall and a spot or two that looked sticky. "You wouldn't think people could get their feet so dirty when it hasn't rained for days. It will take forever to get this clean."

"Let's race. We'll each start at opposite ends of the hall, and the one who gets to the middle first wins." Tommy set his bucket next to Jennie's.

Jennie eyed the long hallway. Usually they helped their mother or older sister Trudy mop, and that meant that it took forever since they both insisted on a careful washing and rinsing of the floor. Jennie had often thought mopping could be done in less time, and she was sure she could win the race with Tommy.

"Let's go!" Jennie yelled. She grabbed her bucket and mop and scurried for the far end of the hall. She mopped feverishly, but still her progress toward the middle seemed turtlelike. Rinsing and wringing out the mop every few minutes took a long time. There must be an easier way to do this.

The first and second time that Jennie glanced down the hall at her brother, he was about as far from the middle as she was; but the third time she looked, he was much farther along. Jennie stretched her neck to get a better view. He had abandoned his mop and was scooting along on his knees, scrubbing at the floor with a brush and some rags. And was he ever going fast!

Jennie frowned. She wasn't about to let her brother win this race. She looked at the stretch of floor in front of her. The part that took so long was the wringing out of the mop. Maybe she should stop wringing it out. She poured a little of the water on the tile, rubbed it around, and moved on. The water flew as she tried to go faster and faster. She slopped and mopped, slopped and mopped. Before long the hall floor behind her glistened with a sheen of water. *Maybe too much water,* she thought when she glanced back, but she figured it would soon dry.

Tommy sped up, too, but Jennie could see that she was gaining on him. Gaining, that is, until a tall blond-haired woman flung open the door to her room and stepped into the hall. She slipped on the wet floor but was able to catch herself by grabbing at Jennie. Jennie promptly staggered into her bucket, dumping the contents. Jennie and the woman stared as the water spread out before them in a tiny tidal wave.

Mama picked that moment to walk around the corner. "What in the world is going on?" The water lay in a big puddle.

"Um, we're mopping," Jennie said and held out her mop for proof. Tommy inched around the edge of the puddle to stand by his sister.

"That's not what I would call this," Mama replied crisply. She stared down the hallway. "It looks like you poured water and sloshed it around."

Jennie remained silent. The blond-haired woman smiled at her and tiptoed through the water to the lobby with Mama apologizing the whole time.

"Now you two get this cleaned up. Pronto."

"I didn't do it," Tommy protested, but Mama gave him a look that made him be quiet.

"Tommy didn't do it," Jennie said. "I managed it all by myself."

"I'm glad you're honest, but he can still help clean up." Mama raised a hand to keep Jennie from talking. "Experience with you two has shown me that if one is in trouble, the other one usually has something to do with it."

Jennie sighed and leaned over to pick up Tommy's bucket.

"I'm off now to volunteer at the ration board," Mama said. "This hallway better be shining clean and dry when I return."

"It will be. I promise," Jennie said. The two spent the better part of the next hour mopping and wiping and polishing. Jennie thought the floor had never looked so good.

She had barely enough time to get cleaned up and changed into her Girl Scout uniform before Colleen arrived. They always walked to the meetings together, carrying burlap bags of crushed tin cans that they had collected since the last meeting. Sometimes they made another stop or two, looking for cans to fill their bags to the very top. Their troop was way ahead of most of the other troops in Seattle in the amount of scrap they had collected.

"How much tin do you think it takes to make an airplane wing?" Colleen asked as they loaded their bags of crushed cans into Jennie's wagon in the alley behind the hotel.

"More than we have here, that's for sure," Jennie replied.

"More than they had at the collection center last week after we took all our cans?"

"Probably." Jennie grabbed the handle of the wagon and pulled, while Colleen pushed and steadied the wobbly bags. They had gone only a few feet when Jennie stopped. "Wait, I forgot to get Mr. Romano's cans. He always has some." The older man lived in a small apartment in the hotel just like Jennie and her family.

"You go," Colleen said. "I'll watch our cans. We don't want any Boy Scouts stealing them." She grinned. The Boy Scouts collected tin cans, too, and Jennie and Colleen were always teasing Tommy and his friend, Stan, saying that the girls could collect more than the boys could.

"I'll be right back," Jennie promised. Mr. Romano's apartment was small with only a living room, a bedroom, and a tiny bathroom. He cooked on a little stove that sat right in his living room. In spite of being small, Mr. Romano's home was overflowing with plants and flowers that he grew in pots. It was a cheerful, sunny place, just like Mr. Romano himself.

"It's my friend Jennie," Mr. Romano boomed as soon as the apartment door swung open. Out of the room drifted the scratchy sounds of a record player. Mr. Romano had been born in Italy and loved Italian opera, which he played endlessly on his old record player. Mr. Romano was an American citizen now, and his son was serving in the Pacific with the navy. That left him with no family any closer than New York City. "What can I do for you? Or perhaps you came for a little visit and a bite of biscotti?"

"Sounds great, but I have to get to my Girl Scout meeting," Jennie said. Mr. Romano made wonderful treats that he liked to share. Even Jennie's mother was amazed at what the man could cook in spite of all the food shortages and rationing. "Do you have any tin cans for crushing?"

"Indeed I do have some for you." He bustled over to a cabinet, pulled out a paper bag, and handed it to Jennie. "I washed them and took off the bottoms, but I left the crushing to you." He grinned.

"Thank you, Mr. Romano," Jennie said. Her neighbor knew that the children liked to jump on the cans and flatten them, so Mr. Romano always left his cans intact. "I better go."

"Oh, by the way. I'm expecting an air raid warning drill any night now, so be ready," Mr. Romano said. Jennie's neighbor was the air raid warden for the block where the hotel sat. He was in charge of making sure that everything went smoothly during the drills. He took his duties very seriously, and more than one resident on the block had received a lecture from him when their blackout curtains weren't closed properly. Any light showing outside a house or apartment was forbidden when the air raid sirens sounded.

Jennie had just turned to leave when Mr. Romano's bedroom door burst open. A large man stood there with his dark hair going every which way. Puzzled, Jennie stared because the man looked so familiar.

"I'm trying to sleep. First it's that caterwauling music, and now you're having a party out here. Can't you keep it down?"

Mr. Romano shook his head and smiled broadly. He seemed unconcerned at the stranger's words or his sudden appearance. "I'm glad you're awake, Pietro. You can meet my friend Jennie. Her family is running this hotel for the owners, the Tanakas."

"Jennie, this is my cousin, Pietro Contadino," Mr. Romano explained.

Pietro nodded at Jennie. "So Japs own this hotel, huh?"

"They are Japanese-Americans," Mr. Romano said. Jennie saw a hint of fire in the old man's eyes. "The same as we are Italian-Americans."

"Right," Pietro said. Jennie had the feeling that Pietro only said what he knew was expected of him. Jennie tried to be polite, but she wanted to stare at Mr. Romano's cousin. Where had she seen this annoying man before?

"Pietro just arrived in Seattle today from New York City. He has come to work in the shipyard and will live with me until he can find his own place." Mr. Romano's smile returned. "It's good to have someone to cook for again."

The cousin's sleep-lined face perked up. "Speaking of cooking," he said, "can a guy get some food around here?"

"Coming right up." Mr. Romano bustled over to his kitchen area.

After a quick good-bye, which Pietro ignored, Jennie escaped with her cans. She frowned as she hurried downstairs to the alley.

She must be mistaken about Pietro looking familiar if the man had just arrived in Seattle today.

Colleen sat on the back step, but she stood when Jennie burst out the door. Something flashed through Jennie's brain, and she remembered where she had seen Mr. Romano's rude cousin. Pietro Contadino was the man she had run into after the plane crash. He was the man who had mumbled foreign words and then ignored Jennie. But that was days ago. Why had Pietro told Mr. Romano that he had only arrived today? Why was he lying? There was something fishy going on with that fellow, but what?

CHAPTER 3

Sliding into Trouble

Colleen was all ears when Jennie told her about Pietro and his claim to have arrived in Seattle just that morning. In fact, Colleen said the girls should march back up the stairs to demand the truth from Mr. Romano's cousin.

Jennie shook her head at that idea. She wasn't sure what to do, but facing Pietro right now didn't appeal to her. All during the Girl Scout meeting Jennie kept thinking about the stranger. Could she have mistaken Pietro for some other dark-haired man?

At last the meeting was over, and the scouts gathered up their sacks and boxes of cans to cart off to the collection center. Jennie and Colleen joined the parade with their wagonload and cheered with the others as the pile of crushed cans towered higher.

"I still think that's enough tin for an airplane wing," Colleen said. The friends stood back a little from the pile. "Don't you?"

Jennie didn't answer.

"Jennie, don't you?" Colleen repeated and shook her friend's arm.

"Oh, sorry," Jennie replied. "I was thinking about something else."

"Are you thinking about that Pietro character? I still think we should go right up to him and ask him why he lied." Colleen put the empty sacks in the wagon and grabbed the handle.

"I've thought and thought, and I'm positive that it was him last week." Jennie shoved her hands in her pockets and walked beside Colleen, who pulled the wagon. Jennie had always been able to remember faces better than anyone else in her family, and this time was no exception.

"So let's go find him," Colleen insisted.

"No, if he's up to something, it might scare him off," Jennie said. "We'll just keep an eye on him. See what we can find out."

"How will we do that?" Colleen asked.

"He lives in the hotel. Shouldn't be too hard."

Since Jennie was helping a lot at the hotel, it was Wednesday after school before she got a chance to check up on Pietro and Mr. Romano. Wednesday was the day that Jennie and Tommy usually collected waste fat from people who lived in the hotel's apartments. Jennie thought it was the worst smelling job of the war, but the fat could be used to make ammunition. She held her nose when possible and reminded herself that these bullets might save Roger.

Jennie and Tommy took turns carrying a big can into which people dumped their smaller cans of collected fat. After they made their rounds, they took the nearly full can of fat to the butcher's shop, which was the official collection center. At least that was what they used to do. Jennie had decided last week that she and Colleen would collect fat themselves. That way they could contribute the pennies they were paid for the fat to their Girl Scout troop's war bond fund.

So today Jennie was collecting on her own, which suited her

fine. That way she could visit with Mr. Romano and find out more about Cousin Pietro.

"Mr. Romano," Jennie called after knocking on her neighbor's door. It would be unusual for the older man to be gone this time of day, but there was no answer to Jennie's repeated knocking.

She was just about to turn and leave when the door opened. The older man peeked out and opened the door wider when he saw Jennie.

"I came to collect your fat," Jennie said, "just like usual." Jennie waited for the usual jovial response from her friend, but Mr. Romano's tired-looking face barely creased into a smile.

"Oh yes," Mr. Romano said. "I forgot this was Wednesday. Come on in, Jennie." He shuffled over to the stove.

Jennie looked curiously at Mr. Romano. She had never known the neighbor to forget any detail. In fact, his memory and love of details had earned the old gentleman some teasing, which he seemed to enjoy.

"Where's your opera?" Jennie asked. The apartment was quiet, too quiet for Jennie's taste. She didn't understand a word of the operas that Mr. Romano played on his record player, but she liked the sounds and the way Mr. Romano would occasionally burst into song, singing along with the record.

"It was too loud for Pietro. He works the night shift at the shipyards. Besides, I was getting tired of the same old music."

Jennie couldn't keep her eyebrows from rising. Mr. Romano, tired of opera? That didn't seem possible. "Are you all right?" Surprised, Jennie blurted out the question.

At last Mr. Romano gave his normal deep rumbling laugh. "I'm just fine. Maybe a bit tired, what with the new routine. You know,

Pietro being here and him needing to sleep in the daytime. It's a change, but I'll be fine." He carefully poured his can of grease into Jennie's larger can. "There you go."

"Does Pietro like his new job?" Jennie asked. Maybe this was the time to get a little more information about the mysterious cousin.

"I think so," Mr. Romano said. "He hasn't said otherwise."

"Did he work in a shipyard back East?"

"I'm not sure. We haven't talked too much about that yet." Mr. Romano put his empty can back on the stove.

"Now you have family here again," Jennie said.

"Yes, I do like that," Mr. Romano said. He shook his head, and his smile faded briefly. "Pietro's not much like the rest of my family, but he needs a place to stay."

Before Jennie could ask any more questions, the bedroom door opened to reveal Pietro dressed for work in dark blue pants and shirt.

"Well, well, if it isn't our little chatterbox from the other day." Pietro smiled at Jennie, but it wasn't the kind of smile that made her want to smile back. "You're still collecting, I see. What is it this time?"

"Fat for making ammunition." Jennie held up her can.

Pietro reached for a pair of gloves lying on the table and jammed them in his pocket. "All this collecting of everything is a waste of time. You can't tell me that some poor sap's leftover bacon grease is worth anything. All those piled-up newspapers and tin cans are just as worthless. The government is sure pulling the wool over your eyes."

"They do so use that stuff," Jennie said loudly. "My father said that fat makes glycerin, which helps make ammunition. He says that if we didn't collect all that scrap rubber and tin cans and such, his job designing airplanes would be much harder. He would have to design them to use less metal and rubber, and that would be really hard." Jennie frowned at Pietro.

"So your father designs airplanes at Boeing, does he?" Pietro asked. "That's interesting."

Jennie's face felt warm, and she had a sudden urge to bolt out the door. "I can't say exactly what he does. He works in a factory, that's all." Now she'd done it. The last thing she should do was tell a stranger that her father designed airplanes at Boeing. That kind of talk was downright dangerous. Pietro had been so aggravating, saying what he did about the collections, but still, Jennie knew that nobody was supposed to talk about war-related factories.

Pietro chuckled in a mean way and pushed open the door to leave. He leaned back in to say, "You'll have to tell me more about your father's job when we have the time."

Jennie wanted to sink out of sight through the floor, she felt so guilty.

"Don't mind him," Mr. Romano spoke up, "he's just kidding." The old man walked over to his record player and turned it on. The opera he had so recently said he was tired of began to play. In a moment Mr. Romano broke into song himself.

Jennie grinned in spite of all the rotten feelings churning inside her. Her friend seemed restored to his old self. What had made the change? In a couple minutes, Jennie began to feel better herself. Maybe Pietro had just been teasing, and after all, everyone in the neighborhood already knew that Father worked at Boeing. Maybe she hadn't done anything that was so awful, but she knew that she would be more careful in the future. And she knew there was more to find out about Pietro.

It was almost five o'clock by the time Jennie left Mr. Romano's apartment with her can of fat. She'd have to hurry to make her last few stops and still get to the butcher's shop before it closed. No matter what Pietro said, Jennie knew it was important to collect fat and scrap metal and rubber. Finally she was finished, except for Mrs. Parker. She and Tommy always left that neighbor for last because the lady was often cross and made it seem like they were making large sums of money by selling her small amount of grease. Jennie paused in the hallway. With much arguing, Jennie and Tommy had divided up the neighbors when she decided to collect fat on her own, but Mrs. Parker hadn't been assigned to either.

After some thought, Jennie went toward Mrs. Parker's door. Before Jennie could knock, Tommy and Stan appeared behind her.

"Wait a minute," Tommy said. "Mrs. Parker is ours." He carried a can that Jennie could see was almost full of fat. It was fuller than hers was by an inch or two.

"Who says?" Jennie stepped in front of Mrs. Parker's door.

"I say so." Tommy shoved up closer. "We divided up these apartments."

"We forgot Mrs. Parker," Jennie said, "and I got here first. So I get her fat."

"That's not fair," Tommy said. "Is it, Stan?" The other boy looked unsure but shook his head.

"You already have your can almost full," Jennie said, trying a different approach with her brother. "If I get hers, we'll be even." It wasn't that the fat was so important to Jennie, but lately Tommy always had to win everything. It seemed like he was usually one step ahead of her, too. But not this time. That can of fat that Mrs. Parker saved on the back of her counter was Jennie's, fair and square, and she meant to have it.

"We have more in our can because we worked harder," Tommy said. "We even went down the street to two other places."

"That wasn't part of the deal," Jennie said. "We just divided up our old route."

"Stan and I made the route bigger, that's all."

Mrs. Parker's apartment door flew open. The middle-aged woman stood, frowning, with her hands on her hips. "What is all the ruckus out here? You children are as noisy as a herd of elephants."

"We came to collect your fat." Jennie and Tommy spoke at the exact same time and then gave each other dirty looks.

"Well, why didn't you say so instead of standing out here snipping at each other?" Mrs. Parker disappeared into her apartment without inviting them in and reappeared shortly, carrying a small tin. "I should be turning this in myself," she grumbled. "Heaven knows, I could use the money. You children probably spend the money on bubble gum."

"No, ma'am," Jennie said. "All of the money goes to buy war bonds or stamps." She wanted to say more but didn't. As if there were bubble gum to be bought with the few pennies the fat brought. She hadn't had a piece of gum since Christmas, and before that it had been months. The sugar shortage took care of that.

"Here, I'll take that," Tommy said and put out his hand to take Mrs. Parker's can. At the same time he handed his can to Stan.

Jennie turned sharply toward her brother to protest, causing her grip to slip on her own greasy can. She jerked her other hand up to steady it and bumped Stan, who had been leaning forward to take Tommy's can. He in turn lurched into Tommy.

In a blink all three cans were airborne. The oily contents squirted everywhere, including down the front of Mrs. Parker's housedress. The cans clattered to the hall floor, spewing the fat.

All was silence for a split second, and then Mrs. Parker shrieked.

"You horrible children," she yelled after catching her breath.

Doors in the hallway popped open as tenants checked on the source of the commotion. On seeing Mrs. Parker, most of them retreated without a word.

Jennie couldn't move. Fat dripped from her hair to her nose to her shirt. She stared at Tommy, who had a big glob of grease slowly sliding down his cheek. Stan had escaped the worst of the flow and stood with greasy hands outstretched. Jennie thought Stan was trying hard to keep from laughing but was about to fail.

Mrs. Parker continued to complain loudly about ungrateful, ill-behaved, modern children as she backed into her apartment and slammed the door behind her. Jennie looked at the pool of fat on the floor. What should she do now?

That problem was solved when Art and Trudy walked up, keeping a safe distance from their slippery younger brother and sister.

"How in the world did you manage this?" Art asked.

"Pee–uu," Trudy said while holding her nose, "that stuff stinks."

"Oh, be quiet and hand us some rags and the mops," Jennie said. She stepped forward but slipped. Tommy reached out to catch her but then slipped, too.

In a flash they both landed on the floor in a tangle of arms and legs. Jennie looked at her brother, whose nose ended up only a foot away from hers. That nose glistened in the light, and his hair looked like a wet mop. She knew that she must look the same. She heard a muffled sound and looked at Tommy again. He was laughing. She wanted to be mad at him, but she couldn't when he laughed like that. So Jennie did the only thing she could do. She laughed, too.

CHAPTER 4

The Secret Weapon

Jennie, Tommy, and Stan spent a long time scrubbing the hallway floor clean of grease. After they finished, Mama insisted that they take their share of a rare batch of cookies to Mrs. Parker as a peace offering. Jennie hated to miss the cookies, but Mrs. Parker's stern face relaxed a great deal when Jennie handed the lady the plate of cookies.

In the end, the whole mishap was almost worth the trouble, because it made a great story to write to Roger. Jennie included the whole tale in a letter she wrote to their brother, reading it to Tommy before she stuffed the thin sheets into an envelope.

Jennie was worried about Roger. Every day the newspapers carried bad news about the war in Europe, and radio announcers sounded mournful as they reported German U-boat attacks on American ships in the Atlantic Ocean. They hadn't had a letter from Roger in weeks.

By the end of March, Mama turned pale every time she heard the bicycle bell of the telegram messenger. Her volunteer work at the rations board brought her into contact with too many people who had received the dreaded telegrams announcing that a soldier was injured or missing or, worst of all, killed in action.

The family knew little about Roger's exact whereabouts, but

they knew he was in North Africa with a tank unit. Jennie and Tommy sometimes talked to each other about their big brother and how scared they were for him, but to Mama they gave only smiles and hugs. When Jennie was especially worried, she went down the street to the mission and sat in the back of the little chapel. She prayed for Roger and all the other soldiers. Jennie knew that she could pray anywhere, but the quiet chapel soothed her fears.

Jennie and Tommy were busy with school and war efforts and the endless work at the hotel. Jennie usually had so much work to do that she could push her worries about Roger to the back of her mind.

Pietro wasn't around the hotel much, although he still lived with Mr. Romano. Everyone else seemed to think Pietro was just a little rude, but Jennie thought it was more than that. She kept an eye on Pietro whenever she could. She didn't think anyone could be too careful during wartime.

Eventually Pietro changed to the day shift, and Mr. Romano went back to his opera-singing, cheerful self. Having Pietro gone in the daytime seemed to suit Mr. Romano, although he never complained.

April arrived, and with it came spring as well. Mother said that Jennie and Tommy must have spring fever, since they argued and fought with each other so often. Jennie tried to ignore her brother when he was bossy, but sometimes she just had to argue with him.

That arguing landed her on the front stairs of the hotel with a bucket of cleaner and scrub brush one Saturday morning. Mama had banished Jennie to the steps and Tommy to the laundry room to fold towels. The sun was shining outdoors, and the street bustled with activity. Jennie would rather have been playing outside with Colleen, but if she had to work, this wasn't as bad as doing laundry.

"What's this? Have we a new scrubwoman here?" Aunt Irene's voice interrupted Jennie's vigorous scrubbing.

The Flemings called their neighbor Aunt Irene even though she wasn't really their aunt. With all their relatives back in Minnesota, it was fun to pretend that the kind woman was truly an aunt. Aunt Irene had moved to the hotel last fall after her son shipped out to the Pacific.

Jennie leaned back and grinned. "I'm in trouble again."

"Surely not," Aunt Irene said. "Not you or that lively brother of yours, if I were guessing."

"It was all Tommy's fault," Jennie began.

"Don't want to hear it." Aunt Irene held up her hand. "I'm sure there's plenty of blame to go around. What you two need is a new project, and I've had an idea."

Jennie jumped to her feet, sending the scrub brush tumbling down the steps. Aunt Irene always had great ideas. Sometimes it didn't seem like she thought like an adult at all. "What is it?"

"First we have to find Tommy," Aunt Irene said. "Do you know where he is?"

Jennie nodded. "He's in the laundry, but I'm not supposed to get within ten feet of him."

Aunt Irene shook her head in mock despair. "Your poor mother has had all she can take, I see."

"I think so." Jennie smiled again, but this time it was sheepish.

"You keep scrubbing while I talk to your mother. Maybe we can give her some relief."

Jennie scrambled to pick up her scrub brush while Aunt Irene went in the hotel entrance. Jennie finished the stairs as fast as possible and toted her bucket back inside. She could see Aunt Irene and Mama in the hotel office near the front door. Both women were laughing, which Jennie took to be a good sign. In a minute Aunt Irene came out, gestured to Jennie to follow, and walked across the lobby and down the hall to the laundry room.

Tommy was stacking clean towels on a shelf when Jennie and Aunt Irene entered. He looked surprised to see them but very glad to be interrupted.

"Tommy, I want you and Jennie to come with me. I have a new project in mind, but I'll need your help." Aunt Irene turned and marched back toward the stairs. She seemed to take for granted that Jennie and Tommy would follow. Tommy gave Jennie a questioning look, but she could only shrug her shoulders to show that she didn't know what Aunt Irene was up to, either. The two hurried to catch up to their neighbor.

Aunt Irene led them down the sidewalk, past the second-hand store and the barbershop, and around the corner by the cigar shop. They trailed behind her until she stopped abruptly in the middle of the next block. "Here we are." She spread her arms wide.

Jennie looked around in confusion. They stood in front of the vacant lot where some children played. A building had burned there years before and had never been rebuilt. The grass was sparse, but the ground was level and made a pretty good baseball field. Across the street were the butcher shop and a dry goods store.

Tommy spoke first. "What do you mean?" He looked as puzzled as Jennie felt.

Aunt Irene laughed and waved her hand at the lot. "It's perfect for a Victory garden. In fact, there's room for a whole lot of Victory gardens."

Jennie looked at their baseball field and gulped. "A garden? Here?"

"Why, of course," Aunt Irene replied. "President Roosevelt has asked us to grow as much of our own food as possible. This is our chance to do just that."

"But we don't know anything about growing stuff," Jennie said.

"That's the beauty of my idea," Aunt Irene said. "I do know about growing vegetables. I'm from Oklahoma. We raised a lot of our own food when I was growing up." She walked across the lot, talking as she went. "I was passing by this lot earlier today when I had my inspiration. Then, of course, I thought of you two and what hard workers you are."

"This field could be divided up into lots of little gardens. People could grow what they wanted in their own garden," Tommy said.

"Exactly." Aunt Irene beamed. In a moment she turned and proceeded across the lot again, talking with every step.

"But what about. . ." Jennie stopped speaking. She wanted to ask about their baseball games. Jennie liked playing baseball—more than some of the boys did. She watched Aunt Irene and Tommy walk on what had been second base. That kind of question might seem downright unpatriotic right now, not to mention a little selfish. Mentally she said good-bye to a summer of baseball games. Besides, this gardening thing might be fun.

In a few days the whole neighborhood buzzed about the Victory garden. Jennie and Tommy, together with Colleen and Stan, spread the word. Many people wanted to do as the president asked. Aunt Irene said there was no time to spare now that it was April. Gardens should be planted right away to make the most of growing weather.

The following Saturday the vacant lot teemed with gardeners carrying every sort of digging tool. Dad had made a special trip back to their house on Queen Anne Hill; it was being rented to another family while the Flemings ran the hotel. He had rummaged around in the shed until he found an old shovel and hoe and carried them back.

Jennie and Colleen had decided to share a small plot, while Tommy and Stan did the same nearby. They were all excited until Jennie dug into the dirt with the shovel the first time. It only went in a couple of inches. "Must have hit a hard spot," Jennie said to Colleen and moved over a few inches to try again. Still the shovel barely bit into the ground. In a few minutes Colleen tried her luck, but every inch of the ground was rock hard.

Jennie heard grunts of effort and murmurs of complaint from every part of the lot. Backs not used to digging were soon aching as the gardeners scraped and scratched away at the dirt.

"How in the world will we ever get this ground dug up enough to plant anything?" Colleen asked.

Jennie didn't know, so she kept quiet. This gardening was lots harder than Aunt Irene had made it sound.

A commotion in the street attracted everyone's attention. Jennie saw a battered old pickup truck pull to the side and park. A homemade-looking trailer was hooked to the back of the truck, but it wasn't the trailer itself that made Jennie look twice. It was the occupants. Two horses stood placidly chewing on wisps of hay, their heads hanging over the high board sides of the trailer. An old gentleman climbed out of the truck and pulled the pegs on the trailer gate.

Jennie's eyes grew round, and she dropped her shovel so she could run to the street with the others close behind. The man was unloading the horses. Aunt Irene appeared from the other side of the trailer and began giving directions to several men who stood on the sidewalk. They nodded and went to the back of the pickup. Jennie craned her neck but could only see that there was some sort of equipment or machine in the pickup bed. She ran to Aunt Irene.

"What's going on? What are the horses for?" Jennie asked.

"You'll see." Aunt Irene smiled. "We're about to garden Oklahoma-style."

In fifteen or twenty minutes the horses were harnessed and backed up to the equipment that looked a little like a big butter knife turned sideways.

"What is it?" Tommy asked. He stood at Jennie's elbow along with Stan and Colleen.

"It's a plow," Colleen said. "I've seen my uncle use one on his farm."

"Oh yeah," Jennie said, "now I see. I've never looked at a real one."

"Well, I don't see," Stan said. "What does it do?"

"It'll dig up this hard dirt quicker than you can say scat," Colleen said.

Sure enough, in a few minutes the old gentleman yelled, "Ye-ho!" The horses obediently leaned into the harness, and the plow bit into the ground as they pulled it forward. Behind the plow a furrow of brown earth turned over to the sun for the first time in many years.

A cheer rose from the assembled gardeners as they ran to pick up their tools from the lot. The farmer walked beside his horses, guiding them with long reins that trailed along the ground. Another man gripped the handles of the plow and steered as the horses pulled it back and forth across the former baseball field.

Jennie just shook her head and watched. How in the world had Aunt Irene managed to find a farmer with a plow in the middle of Seattle? It was a couple of hours before she could ask her question. By then the plowing was finished, and Jennie caught up with Aunt Irene as she helped two older women mark off their sections. "You just have to know the right people," she answered. "The man with the plow is my good friend's brother. She goes to my church. That's her, over there."

A gray-haired woman wearing a huge hat worked nearby. She had her arms around a small boy, helping him chop at a clod of dirt with a hoe. Her face was wreathed with smiles, and Jennie found herself smiling, as well. The April sun was warm on the back of her neck, and a breeze ruffled her hair. The war seemed far away right now.

Jennie and Colleen worked on their small parcel of ground. They hoed and raked until the dirt was smooth. By the middle of the afternoon, they had run out of steam and lay stretched out on the soft bed of earth. Nearby, Tommy and Stan were giving their garden a final raking.

Jennie turned her head a little to sniff the cool dirt. It had a fresh kind of woody smell. The sun was still shining, and she felt like taking a nap right in the middle of the garden.

"Look what I found." A voice accompanied the shadow that

passed over Jennie. She shaded her eyes and saw Trudy waving a piece of paper.

"What?" Jennie asked and reluctantly sat up.

"Come over here and look at this," Trudy called to Tommy and Stan. The two boys dropped their rakes and walked down the narrow path between gardens.

"What have you got, Trudy?" Tommy called.

"Let's see." Jennie snatched at the paper, but Trudy was too quick and yanked the paper and held it high.

"Not so fast," Trudy said. "Everyone gets to look at it." She put the paper at their eye level.

It was a flyer. Jennie read aloud, "Victory Garden Competition. Enter now. Cash prizes for the best sweet corn, tomatoes, beets, carrots, and cucumbers. To be judged by a competent jury on August 9. Sponsored by the South Seattle Neighborhood Association."

"I saw it at the grocery store." Trudy passed the flyer to Jennie so they could read it again.

In a few moments Jennie looked up from reading. Her eyes shone with pleasure. "We can enter. The entry fee is only twenty-five cents. I have that much."

"So do I," Colleen said.

"So do I," Stan and Tommy said at the same time.

"Let's all enter," Stan suggested.

"We can make it boys against the girls," Jennie announced with a snap of her fingers. "We'll enter as partners."

"You two enter your plot, and Stan and I will enter ours," Tommy said.

"Right." Jennie looked at Colleen, matching grins spread across their faces.

"Sounds great to me," Tommy said. "Stan?"

"I'm in," Stan answered.

"Now wait a minute," Trudy said. "You'd better watch out. Jennie and Tommy have been in trouble before for trying to outdo each other. Why can't you enter the best of both gardens? If you actually manage to grow anything, that is." She gazed pointedly at the bare dirt in front of them, dirt that was a long way from producing prizewinning vegetables.

"It'll be friendly competition. Right, Tommy?" Jennie grinned.

"Sure, friendly only," Tommy agreed. "It'll just add to the fun if we have our own contest."

"I don't know." Trudy frowned and shook her head slowly. "You two never seem to be able to have a friendly competition about anything."

"You just wait," Tommy said. "This time will be different."

"Different," Jennie echoed. Already her brain was clicking along, thinking how she and Colleen could grow the best vegetables. *It should be easy to beat the boys,* she reasoned. *After all, Colleen said she helped her uncle on the farm. Colleen probably knows all there is to know about gardening.* As soon as Trudy walked away, Jennie turned to Tommy.

"We're going to beat the socks off you," she said.

"Is that so?" Tommy shook his head. "When did you get to know so much about gardening? I bet we'll leave you standing in that dirt without a single vegetable to enter in the contest."

"That's what you think," Jennie replied, "but you'll be wrong. We have a secret weapon, an expert." She picked up her hoe and looked at Colleen, who gazed back expectantly.

"And who might that be?" Tommy asked.

"Why, Colleen here, of course," Jennie said. "She knows tons about gardening. Our cucumbers will be a foot long and our tomatoes almost that wide across." She glanced at Colleen, who looked astonished. "We'll definitely win prizes and beat you two," Jennie ended with a flourish of her hoe.

Meanwhile, Colleen had stepped closer to Jennie. "What are you talking about?" Colleen hissed in Jennie's ear.

"We'll just see about that." Tommy stomped off toward the boys' garden and Stan followed.

When the boys were safely out of earshot, Colleen shook Jennie's arm. "I repeat," Colleen said, "what are you talking about? Me! An expert?"

"You said you helped your uncle on his farm," Jennie said. "You know, with the plowing." A mild twinge of concern ran through Jennie. Colleen wasn't acting like an expert.

"I said I saw a plow on my uncle's farm." Colleen ran her hands through her hair. "I was five years old, and my uncle moved to Seattle the next winter. I haven't been on a farm since."

"Oh," Jennie said. "I thought you meant you knew about growing things."

"Don't you think I'd have mentioned that before now?" Colleen folded her arms and frowned at Jennie. "After all, we *have* been getting ready to plant a garden."

Jennie hesitated. "I guess I thought you just didn't want to brag. You mean you don't know about raising tomatoes and carrots and that other stuff?"

"All I know is that I like to eat carrots, and I don't like cucumbers except as pickles."

Jennie leaned on her hoe. This was a definite setback. The

boys would be looking for their own secret weapon to beat the girls, especially since Jennie had made such a big deal about Colleen. The girls would just have to find another way. Jennie wasn't about to let Tommy and Stan walk off with any prizes for the best vegetables.

CHAPTER 5

Manure Tea

Planting was scheduled for Monday after school, but rain set in Saturday night and continued all day Sunday. Jennie stared out the window at church during the preacher's sermon and out the apartment window that afternoon. The rain fell in a steady stream. It often rained in Seattle, but this was practically a deluge. The gutters along the street ran full, and the bucket her sister Trudy put out to catch rainwater to wash her hair overflowed. Aunt Irene assured Jennie that it only meant a day or two of delay while the garden dried out, but Jennie didn't want to waste a day of growing time.

Colleen came over Sunday afternoon, and the two friends sat on the old sofa in the hotel lobby and planned their garden. Colleen liked to have things written down, so she had a scrap of brown paper and a stubby pencil.

"I think we should grow tomatoes and cucumbers and carrots," Jennie said. "I hate beets."

"And corn gets too tall." Colleen wrote down their choices.

"We'll have three chances to win the prizes and beat the boys," Jennie said.

"Speaking of beating the boys," Colleen said, "have you had any more bright ideas about how we're actually going to get this stuff to grow?" She reached over to pick up a packet of seeds she had brought from home. "There are barely any instructions."

Jennie took the packet and read the back for a minute before looking up with a frown. "I see what you mean. But don't you think that you just put the seeds in the ground, cover them up with dirt, and they grow?" All the times she had seen Mr. Romano working with his pots of plants, it had seemed so easy. And Mr. Romano had beautiful, healthy-looking flowers and herbs.

"I think it's harder than that," Colleen said.

Jennie stared at the lobby floor and thought. "There must be someone who can help us. I already thought of Aunt Irene, but she said she wasn't getting in the middle of another contest." The girls fell silent as they racked their brains for a solution.

"Hi, there," Mr. Romano called. "You two look mighty thoughtful there. You working on a big problem?" The neighbor had a sackful of groceries in his arms.

Jennie looked at her Italian friend for a moment and then turned slowly to Colleen. Jennie could tell by Colleen's expression that she was having the same idea. Jennie jumped up from the couch. "Mr. Romano, let me carry those for you."

"That's not necessary," Mr. Romano said, "but thanks for offering."

"I insist, because we want to talk to you about that problem we've been thinking over." Jennie succeeded in taking the groceries and motioned for Colleen to come.

Mr. Romano grinned and led the way to his apartment. "Now just what trouble have you girls got yourselves into this time?" He opened his front door and let Jennie and Colleen enter first.

"Not exactly trouble this time," Jennie said, "but we do need some help."

"Let's see what I can do then," Mr. Romano said.

The girls left Mr. Romano's apartment at suppertime, and Colleen hurried home. The next day Jennie and Colleen talked over Mr. Romano's advice. The rain had finally stopped, so the girls met on the playground to talk.

"What did you think about his growing tips?" Colleen asked.

"It didn't sound too hard," Jennie said. "In fact, he made it sound downright easy." If they had the right fertilizer, that is. Mr. Romano called it manure tea, and it sounded nasty, but if that was what it took to grow prizewinning vegetables, then that's what they'd use.

"When are we getting the manure?" Colleen asked.

"I suppose this afternoon after school is as good a time as any since we can't plant until the ground dries out some," Jennie said.

Mr. Romano had told them about a delivery service that had to go back to using horses and wagons for deliveries after their old truck broke down. He said they would have plenty of manure to get rid of.

"Too bad we weren't looking for manure on Saturday morning when the plow horses came to town," Colleen said. "They left plenty of droppings behind that the farmer had to clean up."

Jennie laughed and nodded. "Meet me at the corner at the cigar shop at four o'clock this afternoon."

Colleen saluted, and they both ran for the school door because the bell was clanging.

By the time the girls met, the sun had chased the lingering clouds out of the sky. "This should dry out the garden pretty quick," Jennie said as they fell into step together.

"How will we carry the manure?" Colleen asked.

Jennie whipped a faded cotton sack out of her pocket. "Mama said we could have this old flour sack."

"Did she know what we were putting in it?"

"She didn't ask," Jennie answered, "but she didn't mention wanting it back."

The delivery service's makeshift stable was close to the waterfront. The girls loved that part of Seattle because there was always so much to see. Art had promised to take them sometime to see the underground tunnels that snaked beneath the streets near the waterfront. The tunnels were left over from the last century before the street level had been raised.

But this time, the girls went directly to the delivery service office and asked the woman sitting at a desk if they could collect some manure. She laughed and said she imagined that would be just fine.

"So how do we pick it up?" Colleen asked a few minutes later when they stood in the entry to the horse stalls and stared at the straw on the ground. A good supply of manure was scattered there. Luckily, the horses were out on a delivery.

Jennie looked around. "Good question. Why don't you just use your fingers?"

"No!" Colleen said loudly. "I'm not touching that stuff with my bare hands."

Jennie grinned. "I didn't think so." She looked around again and saw a broken piece of board in the corner. She picked up the board and held it out to Colleen. "Use this."

"Go ahead." Colleen stepped back.

Jennie took the flour bag out of her pocket and squatted down next to a likely looking pile of manure. "Take the bag," she ordered.

Colleen carefully stepped forward and took the bag from Jennie. She held it open.

Carefully Jennie scooped up a small ball of manure and transferred it to the bag. She repeated her actions several times.

"That stuff smells terrible!" Colleen turned her head as far to one side as possible while still holding open the bag.

"It is a little ripe," Jennie agreed. At last she threw her makeshift scoop back into the corner and stood up. "There, we're done. That should make gallons of manure tea."

Colleen stood, holding the bag as far in front of herself as possible.

"Are you going to carry it home that way?" Jennie asked. "You look pretty silly."

"I guess so, because I'm not getting any closer to that stuff."

"Here, give it to me." Jennie took the bag. She held it by the top and kept the contents well away from her legs as she walked. In this way the two gardeners began the trip home.

They had only gone a block or two when Colleen jabbed Jennie in the side.

"What's that for?" Jennie protested as she shifted her smelly burden.

"Quiet," Colleen ordered. "Look over there." She pointed to a group of men clustered in front of a tavern the girls were passing.

Jennie stared at the men, who laughed as they smoked and talked. What was she supposed to see? Her puzzlement ended when she recognized one of the men—a large fellow. It was Pietro.

Jennie looked at Colleen, and they hurried down the street and stepped into a doorway. They peeked back at the men, careful to stay out of sight.

"I thought he was on the day shift now," Colleen said.

"Mr. Romano said Pietro was on twelve-hour day shifts."

"Not today," Colleen said. "Do you think he's skipping work?"

"Maybe," Jennie said. "Dad's always complaining about how many people don't show up for work every day at the factory. He says it slows down the whole factory. I guess the shipyard is probably the same."

"And this is Pietro we're talking about." Colleen peeked back again. "Say, look at his hands."

Jennie looked again. Pietro was tapping the ash off the end of his cigarette. His hand looked red. "What is that?"

"Paint, maybe?" Colleen ventured.

"It doesn't really look like paint." While Jennie watched, Pietro threw his cigarette into the street and went inside the tavern with the other men. "I don't know what that guy is up to. I wonder why he's lying to Mr. Romano."

"Should we tell Mr. Romano that we saw Pietro?" Colleen asked.

The girls started walking down the street again.

"No, I don't think so. It might make him feel bad to know that Pietro wasn't at work." Jennie wished she could find out more about Pietro. Mr. Romano was too nice a man to have a lying cousin hanging around.

It was getting late by the time Jennie and Colleen reached the alley behind the hotel with their smelly bag.

"What will we put the manure tea in?" Colleen asked.

"An old bucket should work," Jennie said. "I forgot to ask if we should put it on once when we plant the seeds or more often than that."

"I don't want to have to go back and collect more manure,"

Colleen said firmly, "so save some of it for later. Put it under that broken crate over there. I'll find a bucket for the tea." Colleen looked around. "It's getting dark. We'd better finish."

Jennie moved the crate aside a little. "There's an old bucket down by the fire escape stairs. Go get it while I dump some of this manure. We'll get water and mix up the whole mess." She held the bag and dumped part of its contents on the ground under the wooden crate.

Colleen returned in a few minutes with a bucket. "Here, this should do it." She handed the bucket to Jennie. "It even had water in it already."

"Good." Jennie took the bucket. "Mr. Romano said to put the manure in a bag into the water." Jennie knotted the top of the flour bag and gingerly poked it in the bucket. It floated until she took a stick and shoved it farther into the bucket.

"I don't see how this will make the vegetables grow," Colleen confessed.

"Mr. Romano said it was like steak and spinach to plants." Jennie poked at the sack some more.

"I have to go home," Colleen said. "Do you leave the sack in the water?"

"I don't know," Jennie said. "I'll have to ask Mr. Romano that, too."

"You better take it out for now," Colleen said, "until you can ask him. It might be too strong if you leave it in there until tomorrow."

"You're right," Jennie agreed. "We wouldn't want to kill our seeds before they even get started." She used the stick to lift out the sopping sack, which was now an unfortunate shade of brown, and scooted it under the crate with the extra manure. The bucket of freshly brewed manure tea was left beside the back hotel door. She'd check with Mr. Romano later to see if she should put the sack back in the water.

Supper was Jennie's wartime favorite—beans and cornbread. She ate until she was stuffed and then sat down to listen to the war news on the radio. Sometimes it seemed like that was all that was on the radio these days, but she knew it was important to know what was happening all those thousands of miles away on the other side of the world. The family gathered around the radio to listen together most evenings.

Except for Trudy, who often skipped that ritual. She said it was almost as hard not to hear any news related to her fiancé, Mike, as it was to hear bad news. Mike Fancher had been missing in action in China for two years.

Jennie noticed Trudy walk past the living room door in their apartment, carrying a bucket. Jennie didn't pay much attention since Trudy was always washing her hair with the rainwater she collected.

The announcer had just signed off when a scream echoed through the apartment. Jennie jumped up, followed by everyone else. The scream had come from the bathroom, and now there were angry noises coming from the same room.

In seconds they all crowded in the open bathroom door. A red-faced Trudy with fire in her eyes stood before them. She was dressed in her bathrobe, and her hair dripped water over her face and robe.

"What's wrong?" Mama asked.

"I started to wash my hair." Trudy waved at the sink. "With my rainwater. The same rainwater that I always collect. In the same bucket." She glared at her family. "But it seems that someone has put some horrible concoction in my bucket without telling me." She held out a strand of her hair. "It smells like. . ." She hesitated as words apparently failed her. "It smells like a barnyard!" she burst out finally.

Jennie backed away from the group. This was as good a time as any to visit Mr. Romano.

"Jennie!" Mama grabbed Jennie's arm.

Jennie smiled as innocently as she could.

"Do you know anything about this little mishap?" Mama asked.

"Sort of. Colleen and I were making manure tea for fertilizer for our garden."

"I put manure tea on my hair?" Trudy shrieked.

Jennie wiggled behind Art, who was laughing uproariously. Trudy tried to grab her little sister, and in the process, the foul-smelling water in her hair flew in droplets over all of them.

"Wait, Trudy," Mama said and glared at Dad, who looked to be holding in laughter, too. "We'll take care of Jennie. You wash your hair."

Jennie peeked out from behind Art. "It's good for plants. Maybe it would be good for your hair, too."

Trudy returned to the bathroom.

"I'm waiting." Mother tapped her foot as she waited for Jennie to go into the living room. "This had better be good."

Jennie grinned. "Oh, it is. It's patriotic, even." She hoped that fertilizer for a Victory garden fell into that area.

Mama just rolled her eyes.

CHAPTER 6

The Victory Garden Contest

"Too bad Mama made you share your secret weapon," Tommy said one hot July day when they arrived at the Victory garden to work in their plots.

"If you've said that once, you've said it a hundred times." Jennie chopped a weed that dared to grow near the tomatoes.

"Without that manure tea, our vegetables probably wouldn't be nearly as big as yours," Tommy said. "You might have won the contest hands down. Too bad that won't happen now." He wiped a pretend tear from the corner of his eye and walked off.

Tommy had been teasing Jennie about the manure tea for weeks now. Trudy had forgiven Jennie long ago, but Tommy wouldn't let her forget it. According to Mama, it wasn't important who had the biggest tomatoes or cucumbers. It was important to do everything possible to help win the war so Roger and Mike and all the soldiers could come home. Apparently Tommy didn't agree.

Both gardens now had large glossy tomatoes and long shiny cucumbers. The boys had planted corn and beets, and Jennie had to admit that the vegetables looked great. Even the carrots were fat and long. Some of the other gardens had vegetables that looked almost as good, but Jennie was convinced that the fertilizer had made the difference.

Actually she had been using one more of Mr. Romano's growing tips. It was more secret than the manure tea. Even Colleen didn't know, but Jennie hoped it would make the difference come judging time. Hoeing finished, she looked around to see if anyone was near before she sat down among the tomato plants to give them a dose of fertilizer. But this time it wasn't manure tea.

"Nancy, you're looking especially fine today," Jennie said in a low voice. "And Oscar, I've never seen you looking so healthy. Mary, your tomatoes have grown since yesterday. Now, all of you just hold on a day or two. Dad says it's bound to rain tomorrow."

A chuckle made Jennie jerk her head. Colleen stood nearby with a puzzled grin.

"What are you doing?" Colleen asked. "Talking to the tomato plants?"

Jennie jumped up. "Quiet!" she ordered before glancing around to see if Tommy was still in his plot. "It's my other secret weapon. Mr. Romano says that he always talks to his plants. He thinks that makes them grow better."

"So you *were* talking to them," Colleen said.

Jennie tilted her head and grinned before nodding. "I gave them names so it wouldn't feel quite so silly. This is Mary and Nancy and Oscar, and the others have names, too."

Colleen looked uncertain whether she should laugh or not. Finally she shrugged and asked, "Do you think it's working?"

"I can't be sure," Jennie said, "but I think so. Some of our tomatoes seem to be growing faster than the boys' tomatoes. Mr. Romano says it works for him. What can it hurt? If you don't tell anyone, that is."

"Oh, I won't be telling anyone that my best friend is sitting in the middle of a tomato patch telling the plants how wonderful they are," Colleen said. She plopped down in the dirt near the cucumbers. "I'm ready. What do cucumbers need to hear to make them grow?"

Jennie laughed and sat next to Colleen. "I usually tell them how shiny and green they're looking, but you don't have to talk to them today. It's not really their turn."

"Whew!" Colleen said. "Thank goodness. I may have to think a little about what to say, especially to the carrots. They're probably more particular than cucumbers. Thank goodness we don't have any sweet corn."

The girls flopped backward in the dirt and laughed.

"What's so funny?" Tommy called and walked down the path to stand over them.

"Oh, nothing," Jennie assured him. She wasn't about to give away another gardening secret to her brother. Colleen got up and went with Tommy to see the boys' vegetables, but Jennie remained where she was. She liked the smell of nearly ripe tomatoes that blended with the aroma of warm dirt.

The Victory garden had helped her not think about the war so much, which was funny since the only reason they had a Victory garden was because of the war. Jennie was glad to hear her parents talk about normal, everyday things like how long before the tomatoes would be ripe, and she liked to argue with her brothers and sisters about the best kind of pickles to make with the cucumbers.

A bundle of letters from Roger had finally arrived in May and twice more since then. He was safe so far, but there were new worries. Just last week the papers had headlined the news that the Allies had invaded Italy. The family couldn't be sure, but it seemed likely that Roger's unit had been part of that action. Jennie rolled on her side and watched as a ladybug crawled up one of Oscar's stems. Jennie prayed for her brother every day, but sometimes she wondered how God handled this war business. What if the Italian and German families were praying for their soldiers to defeat the Americans at the same time that the Americans were praying the opposite? What would God do?

She was finding out that war was more complicated than the good guys against the bad guys like in the movies. The family had received a letter yesterday from the Tanakas. They were still in the internment camp in Idaho. Jennie hadn't been especially close to the Japanese family, but she knew they were loyal Americans. It was hard to understand why they should be locked up.

Mr. Romano's brother still lived in Italy, and Jennie could see that her Italian neighbor was very worried about his brother. Jennie knew that he wasn't one of the bad guys if he was as nice as Mr. Romano. God had His work cut out trying to solve this war mess.

Jennie sat up. It was time to go home and do some chores. She glanced around but saw no sign of Tommy. She leaned over and whispered another encouraging word to Oscar. What could it hurt?

At last August arrived and with it the day of the contest. Jennie and Tommy met Colleen and Stan at the Victory garden early that morning. Aunt Irene had said it would be best to pick everything at the last minute to preserve the freshest taste possible.

Jennie held up a just-picked tomato and yelled across the garden to Tommy, "This one looks like it would taste delicious! It's awfully plump and firm, and would you look at that color?"

"I've got one here that's twice as big, and talk about color," Tommy yelled back, "why it's perfect! And I can tell from the smell that it's going to knock those judges' socks off."

"Why do you two argue all the time?" Colleen asked.

Jennie looked up from picking another tomato. "I don't know," she admitted. "We didn't used to, but now we just do. He always has to be best at everything." It was true. She and Tommy argued a lot more nowadays. She wasn't sure she liked it, but that's the way it was.

At last they all finished picking a good amount of each of their ripe vegetables. They took them to Jennie and Tommy's apartment to wash and choose which ones to put on plates for the judging.

Tommy was hovering over the kitchen sink, lovingly washing each carrot and ear of corn. Jennie stood nearby with Colleen, waiting to use the sink.

"You don't have to take each bit of corn silk off by itself!" she burst out, unable to wait any longer. She kept looking at the clock. If Tommy didn't hurry up, they were going to be late to the contest.

"Oh, don't be such a grouch." Tommy took another ear from Stan who stood nearby. "We want them to be perfectly clean for the judges." With exaggerated care he peered at the ear of corn and plucked nearly invisible strands of corn silk from it. Or at least they looked invisible to Jennie.

"I mean it, Tommy, hurry up." It took a lot to make Jennie angry, but her brother was getting near her limits.

"Jennie, go away and leave us alone. Go to the sink in the laundry room or use the bathroom sink." Tommy continued to pluck at the corn silk. "We still have to wash our tomatoes."

"The bathroom sink is too small, and we don't have time to

traipse over to the laundry room." Jennie's frustration mounted. "Hurry up!" Her words came out loud. Probably louder than she intended. Stan jumped when Jennie yelled and bumped his arm on the boys' tomato basket, which had been resting precariously on the edge of the counter.

The next thing Jennie knew, the tomatoes were spilling out of the basket as it tumbled to the floor. She grabbed for them, but it was too late. They hit the floor and some of them split and splattered juice and seeds everywhere.

"Jennie Fleming," Tommy roared, "you did that on purpose!"

"No, I didn't!" Jennie yelled. "I'm sorry. It was an accident." She got down on the floor to pick up the squishy tomatoes.

"You just want to make sure that you win the contest." Tommy's face was red.

"That's not true. It was an accident," Jennie repeated. "I didn't touch that basket."

"You didn't have to."

"You shouldn't have left it sitting on the edge. It's your fault."

"What's going on here?" A calm voice asked from the kitchen door.

It was Mama, and Jennie knew that tone. It was calm all right, dangerously calm.

It didn't take long for Mama to sort out everything. In a few minutes the law had been laid down. The two were forbidden to enter the contest. If Stan and Colleen wanted to take the vegetables and enter, they could.

"I don't want to hear that kind of ugly talk between my children ever again," Mama said. "If we don't all work together while this terrible war rages, we will not survive. God expects us to love each other and show that love in every way."

Mama walked off down the hall, her heels clicking briskly on the linoleum floor. Jennie and Tommy looked at each other.

"I'm sorry," Jennie said after a moment.

"Me, too," Tommy said.

Jennie plopped down on a kitchen chair. "Now we can't enter the contest."

"I guess it's just as well," Tommy said. "Our tomatoes are ruined."

"Your corn is fine," Jennie pointed out, "and extremely clean."

Tommy grinned. "It sure is."

Colleen and Stan had been talking and now smiled at them.

"We have an idea," Stan said.

"A great idea, in fact," Colleen added.

"Colleen and I will enter the vegetables like your mother said. But we'll just enter tomatoes and cucumbers for the girls and carrots and sweet corn for the boys," Stan said. "That way we might win, but we won't be competing against each other."

"If we had thought of that to start with," Jennie said, "we wouldn't be in so much trouble. Come on. Let's leave, or we're going to miss the whole thing."

The hall was packed with people. Many had entered their prize vegetables, but just as many seemed to have come for the fun of it. It wasn't an ordinary thing to have a vegetable-growing contest in the middle of a big city like Seattle, but then nothing was ordinary during the war.

Jennie sniffed with pleasure as they entered the big basement room. The fresh smells of all the produce blended together to make an aroma that was almost like vegetable soup. Soon the long tables were covered with plates of corn and beets and tomatoes. Cucumbers and carrots sat alongside.

With much laughter and pretend ceremony, the judges entered the hall. There were two men and two women, and Jennie thought she saw their eyes widen when they saw all the entries. They didn't say anything but began working their way down the tables, looking and sniffing and sometimes tasting.

The hall was hot, and after awhile Jennie and Colleen went to find a drinking fountain. They took turns taking long slurps from the fountain in the hall entryway. Jennie glanced out the open door while she waited for Colleen to take one more drink.

On the sidewalk stood Pietro talking to a short, brown-haired man who didn't look a thing like anyone Jennie had ever seen in the neighborhood. In spite of the hot day, the man was dressed in a black suit complete with a necktie and shiny black shoes. Jennie hadn't seen any shoes that new-looking since the war started.

"Look out there," Jennie whispered to Colleen and pointed.

Colleen looked and groaned. "Pietro has more unexpected days off from work than anyone I've ever seen. Too bad our fathers can't get off as often."

The pair outside moved to one side so the girls couldn't see them anymore. "Let's see what they're doing," Jennie suggested. Before Colleen could respond, Jennie walked the few steps to the door.

Pietro and his dressed-up friend were walking across the street toward a drugstore.

"Come on, let's follow them," Jennie said.

"Should we do that?" Colleen hesitated in the doorway.

Jennie chewed her lip for a moment. She knew what her mother would say about snooping, but this was a special circumstance. She was almost sure of that. "That guy with Pietro looks pretty suspicious. You said yourself that Pietro is always off work. We better check them out."

Colleen nodded and they ran across the street to peer in the drugstore window. Pietro and the other man were just sitting down in a booth near the back.

"Come on," Jennie said. "We can pretend to look at the comic books on that rack."

Colleen looked a little alarmed but followed Jennie behind a counter and back to the magazine rack, which was only a few feet from the booth where Pietro and the man sat. Jennie picked up a comic book and held it right in front of her face. Colleen did likewise. They were careful to keep their backs to the two men.

"Everything is coming along just as planned," Pietro said.

"You seem to have the knack for it," the other man said.

A small hand tugged on Jennie's elbow. "I want that comic book."

Jennie ducked her head enough to see that a small boy stood beside her.

"Go away," Jennie said in a low voice. This was no time to attract attention.

"I want that one," the boy repeated loudly and grabbed for the comic book that Jennie held in front of her face. It slipped, and Jennie ducked down as the boy pulled away the comic book. All Jennie could think of was to get out of sight, so she crawled behind the nearby cigarette counter and toward the front of the drugstore. She looked back and saw that Colleen had followed.

At the end of the counter the girls jumped up and dashed out the door. They ran across the street and didn't stop until they were inside the hall once more.

"Do you think they saw us?" Colleen asked.

"I don't think so, but that kid sure messed up things," Jennie said disgustedly. "It was just starting to get good."

"What do you suppose is coming along as planned?" Colleen asked.

"I don't know," Jennie said, "but I wish I could figure it out."

"There you are." Tommy rushed up to the two girls. "Come on. The judges are finished. Let's see if we won a ribbon."

Jennie cast one last glance across the street before hurrying after the boys and Colleen. Checking up on Pietro would have to wait awhile longer.

A red, second-place ribbon sat on the table in the hall on the girls' tomatoes and a red ribbon was on the boys' sweet corn, as well.

"Not bad for beginners," Trudy said when she walked up behind them to join in the admiration.

"Our tomatoes probably would have won. . ." Tommy stopped.

Jennie looked at her brother. "What did you say?"

"Never mind." He grinned. "We did great."

Jennie grinned back. It was the first time in weeks that she didn't feel like arguing with her brother. This time he made sense.

CHAPTER 7

Goats and Floats

Jennie slammed the front apartment door after school one afternoon in September. She sniffed the smell of hot tomatoes.

"Don't slam the door!" Her mom's voice came from the kitchen.

"Sorry!" Jennie tossed her arithmetic book at a nearby chair and ran across the living room to the kitchen door.

"Slow down," Mama ordered from where she stood over a steaming pot at the stove. Her forehead glistened with sweat, and she pushed back a strand of hair that had fallen across her face.

"Yes, ma'am." Jennie flopped in a chair at the kitchen table where a row of glass jars sat. Trudy stood at the table cutting up a big pile of tomatoes, one after another.

"What are you doing?" Jennie asked.

"What does it look like we're doing? What are we doing every day? Canning these awful tomatoes, that's what," Trudy said.

"I'm getting downright sick of the smell of tomatoes. Why do you keep canning them?" Jennie asked, more to tease her sister than because she wanted an answer.

"Come winter, you'll be glad enough to have these canned tomatoes," Mama said tartly. "The food shortages make it harder all the time to find the things we like, and these vegetables will taste good in January."

Jennie looked over at the wooden shelves that Dad had put up in the corner of the crowded kitchen. Jars of bright yellow corn, orange carrots, deep red tomatoes, and purple beets were lined up. She smelled the pickles that Mama was making in a big stone crock near the table. The tomatoes Trudy was slicing would soon be joining the others. It seemed like Jennie's mom and older sister had been canning for weeks.

"Our gardens did good," Jennie said with satisfaction.

"Almost too good," Trudy said.

Jennie grinned. The Victory gardens had produced bushels of vegetables. The corn and beets and carrots were done now, but the cucumbers and tomatoes kept coming. Everyone in the hotel had been well supplied with vegetables. Jennie had taken some tomatoes to Mr. Romano just yesterday. With Pietro to feed, Mr. Romano needed all the help he could get.

Jennie had kept a close eye on Pietro since the contest. Although she hadn't found out a single new thing about the plans the two men had mentioned in the drugstore, she wasn't giving up. Any little bit of information might be a clue, so Jennie was staying alert.

"Why are you so late?" Mama asked. "And where is Tommy?" She poured a glass of milk and placed it with a big slice of bread in front of Jennie.

"Thanks," Jennie replied. "He's talking to Stan. I had an emergency Girl Scout meeting after school."

"Emergency?" Mama questioned.

"Well, not exactly emergency," Jennie admitted. "We wanted to start planning our float for the parade. We think the Boy Scouts are doing a float, too." She took a big bite of bread and followed it with a gulp of milk.

"What parade is that?" Trudy asked.

"The parade for the third war loan drive." Jennie shook her head at her sister's ignorance. There had already been two war loan drives, and Jennie was looking forward to this one. For the other drives there had been rallies and parades and lots of excitement, and this one promised to be the same.

"I see," Trudy said. "So you're making a float."

"It's going to be a humdinger," Jennie said before popping the last of her bread into her mouth.

"No doubt the Boy Scout float will be a humdinger, too," Trudy said.

"Not as good as ours," Jennie insisted.

"I don't want to hear that kind of talk," Mama said. She lowered another canning jar into the kettle of hot water before turning to her youngest daughter. "It's fine to build a float, but it's not fine to spend all your time trying to outdo someone else. The purpose of the parade is to convince people to buy war bonds and stamps, not to dazzle them with a float."

"I know," Jennie said, "but the boys—"

"No buts about it," Mama said firmly. "Before long, you and Colleen will be wanting to impress those boys instead of show them up."

"Not us," Jennie said with a decisive shake of her head. She couldn't imagine wanting to impress a boy. She liked Stan fine, and Tommy was a lot of fun when he wasn't trying to win at something, but Jennie didn't care a thing about impressing either one of them.

The apartment front door burst open and then banged shut.

"Don't slam the door!" Mama called. The words were barely out of her mouth when Tommy ran into the kitchen.

"You won't believe how spectacular the Boy Scout float will be," he announced to everyone before dropping into a chair beside Jennie.

"You're right," Jennie said, "I won't believe it."

"Jennie," Mama warned.

Jennie grinned. "So what will your float look like?"

"I can't tell you," Tommy said. "It's a secret, but it'll be better than what you girls make, that's for sure."

"Tommy," Mama said sharply, "I've just been all through this with your sister. No more competition. Work together for a change."

"But, Mama," Tommy said, "we can't do that. The Boy Scouts want their own float."

"And so do the Girl Scouts," Jennie added.

"Well, fine, but I don't want any arguing, or you two will be sitting out the parade just like the Victory garden contest. Understand?" Mama stared at them until both Jennie and Tommy nodded in agreement.

"Speaking of Victory gardens," Trudy said. "I just cut up the last tomato. Hallelujah!"

Jennie went off to do her chores, but she thought the whole time about the parade. Maybe they couldn't have an official contest, but at least the Girl Scouts could make the best float possible. They needed a good idea, and that wasn't all. A float was usually on a wagon pulled by a tractor or truck. With gas and tire rationing, there weren't many vehicles left to be used for floats. This was going to take some thought.

Jennie couldn't wait to get to school so the girls could huddle together and plan their float. Most of the girls in her class were in

Girl Scouts, and the others liked to give their opinions. School was especially fun this year. Tommy and Stan were in the class behind Jennie, but Colleen was in the same class. Even better, Mrs. Hoffman had changed teaching positions from third to fourth grade, so Jennie had Mrs. Hoffman again. She was young and pretty, and she said learning should be fun. Jennie was sure that she and Colleen had the best teacher in the world.

Mrs. Hoffman gave her class some time almost every day to work on projects related to the war effort. She said their work was just as important as what adults did and that the soldiers said so, too. Jennie thought Mrs. Hoffman should know since her husband was a pilot in the army air corps. Mr. Hoffman's picture sat on Mrs. Hoffman's desk next to her pencil cup. Last year he wrote two letters to their class, and his wife talked about him often.

Mrs. Hoffman had tacked up a big map of the world on one wall of their classroom, and the students had pinned tiny American flags on every place where soldiers they knew served. For a few, the flags represented their fathers, and for others it was brothers or sisters or other relatives. Jennie had carefully pinned up a flag for Roger in Italy and one for Mike Fancher in China.

Some students pinned up little black crosses on the map for soldiers they knew who had died. One student put a cross over Hawaii because his brother had died in the attack on Pearl Harbor. Mrs. Hoffman said it was good to remember those who died, that it helped the pain go away just a little. Jennie was thankful that there were many more flags than crosses on the map. That gave her hope that Roger's and Mike's flags wouldn't have to be changed to crosses.

A week passed, and Jennie was getting worried about the Girl Scouts' float. Every idea they'd had so far didn't work out. One of the troop members had thought she could borrow a farm wagon from her uncle who lived south of Seattle. The girl's uncle said that was fine, but unless the girl wanted to pull it herself, there was no way to get it into Seattle. Her uncle's old truck had long since been parked because the tires were too worn and new ones were hard to get. The uncle's family rode the bus everywhere.

"I don't see how we can make a float when we don't have anything to put it on," Colleen said one afternoon after school while she and Jennie were collecting fat in the hotel again.

"True," Jennie agreed, "but that's not all. If we had a wagon, how would we decorate it? I haven't been able to find any paper that we can use for streamers. All I have is two old posters from the Victory garden contest. We could write on the back of those."

"This war and all the shortages mess up everything," Colleen said.

Jennie nodded. She couldn't argue with Colleen's words. There were exciting things about the war, but mostly it was a lot of trouble and pretty scary.

The friends made a couple more stops to get fat and headed for Mr. Romano's apartment. "Have the boys come up with anything?" Colleen asked.

"I'm not sure," Jennie answered, "but I think so. Tommy and Stan were making a list last night, and all the boys were talking together at recess today."

"They've thought of something," Colleen said glumly, "that's for sure."

"Don't give up," Jennie said. "We'll figure it out. Those boys aren't going to beat us." At least she hoped not. She thought she had heard Tommy tell Mama that Stan's father knew about an old trailer. Another boy said they could use his brother's motorcycle to pull the trailer. If that were so, then the Boy Scouts were halfway to having a real float. It would be small, but small or large didn't matter if you didn't have anything at all to pull a float.

"Hi there." Mr. Romano opened the door and ushered the girls into his apartment. "I'm just getting the dirty clothes ready to take to the Chinese laundry." He inspected a blue shirt he held. "I don't know where in the world Pietro gets these nasty red stains on his work shirts."

"Maybe at work?" Jennie grinned. She took her can over to the stove where she knew Mr. Romano's small fat-collecting can sat.

Mr. Romano chuckled. "Seems likely, doesn't it? Only problem is that Pietro is a welder. He's said before that he wears a heavy leather apron. These stains aren't burns anyhow. They're more like ink." The older man peered again at the shirt in his hand. "Oh well. It doesn't matter. Stains are stains, and these don't come out." He dropped the shirt in a pile of clothes. "What are you two up to these days?"

Jennie motioned for Colleen to steady the big can while she poured the contents of the smaller one into it. "We're trying to make a float for the parade Saturday, but so far we don't have a wagon or anything to put it on."

"And we don't have a good idea, either," Colleen added. "We think the Boy Scouts do, though."

"Always trying to beat the boys, aren't you?" Mr. Romano asked.

"Not much chance of that this time," Colleen said.

"We'll think of something." Jennie took the big can from

Colleen once more. "Any ideas, Mr. Romano?"

"Let's see." Mr. Romano frowned in thought. "Hmm, an idea for a float, you say?"

"Anything at all," Jennie said.

"I wonder if you might not look at the problem from a different direction," the old man said. "Perhaps a float isn't the only possibility—or at least not the wagon or trailer kind of float."

"Like what?" Jennie asked.

"I saw something in a magazine the other day," Mr. Romano said. "Now where did I put that?" He leaned over to rummage in a box that sat by his big chair. In a moment he pulled a magazine out and flipped it open. "Here it is." He pointed to a picture. "I thought this was a great idea for a slogan."

Jennie put down the fat can and crowded close with Colleen to stare at the magazine. The girls saw a picture of several boys with one wearing a Boy Scout uniform. It looked like they were in a parade because they were lined up in a street and carried a big banner. Jennie stared at the banner. It said, "THE AXIS CAN'T GET OUR GOAT. BUY MORE WAR BONDS AND STAMPS." In the midst of the boys stood a goat.

"Wow!" Jennie said. "This is great. We wouldn't need a wagon or anything."

"We'd just dress in our Girl Scout uniforms, kind of like we were soldiers," Colleen said.

"And we could make a big sign with those old posters," Jennie added.

"But where would we find a goat?" Colleen asked and looked glum once more.

Jennie's smile broadened. "I think we can take care of that, too.

Remember how Karen talks about having to drink goat's milk and sometimes she brings goat cheese to school?"

"She hates it." Colleen nodded.

"Her grandmother lives farther south, where she has a little backyard. She keeps a goat in it. We'll borrow her goat for the parade." Jennie went to the door. "Come on, let's go call Karen. Thanks, Mr. Romano."

"Thanks a bunch," Colleen added and followed Jennie.

"You're welcome, girls," Mr. Romano said. "It was nothing."

The girls were in the hall before Mr. Romano called, "Wait— don't forget your can!"

Jennie darted back to pick up the can she had left in the middle of Mr. Romano's floor. "Sorry about that," she said. "Guess I'm kind of excited. The boys sure won't have a goat."

"Probably not." Mr. Romano smiled and shut his door.

"Let's go to the hotel office and call Karen." Jennie hurried down the hall. "I think this will be great."

Jennie was relieved that the goat idea seemed to work out fine. Karen's grandmother said she didn't care if Dody came to town for the big parade. The girls made the sign, found a fake mustache for the girl who was to be Hitler pretending to get their goat, and waited for Friday.

The parade was scheduled for 2:00 p.m., and school was to be let out early for the event. Mrs. Hoffman had a hard time settling down the fourth-grade students so they could take their spelling test that morning.

The Boy Scouts had brought their float to the school playground early on Friday since the parade starting point was nearby. Jennie had to admit that the boys' float was nice. They had used all sorts of tin cans and other scrap to build a shape that looked quite a bit like a tank. When the parade was over, they would haul the float straight to the collection station for recycling.

Everyone who could hurried home at lunchtime to put on costumes or bring other items for the parade. Right before the bell rang, the girls all met in a corner of the playground to be sure they had everything.

"Hey, girls," a breathless voice yelled. Jennie turned to see Karen pulling at a rope attached to a brown and white goat that didn't seem too excited about being led across the playground. The animal stopped every few feet and refused to budge until Karen tugged and held out a piece of grass. Then the goat would walk another few steps, stop, and repeat the process.

Jennie, Colleen, and the others ran up to Karen and the goat. "I thought your sister was going to bring Dody right before the parade," Jennie said.

"She got called in to work," Karen said, "and my mother said she wasn't touching this ornery goat. Since my uncle brought Dody from Grandma's this morning, she's already chewed up one side of my mother's clothes basket and the corner of a sheet." Karen raised her hands in defeat. "I had to bring her with me."

"We'll tie her up to the fence in the shade over there." Jennie pointed across the graveled playground to near where the Boy Scout float was parked, waiting for the parade. "Quick, before the bell rings, run and pull her some grass to eat."

Colleen and a couple other girls ran toward a patch of grass in front of the school.

"Come on, Dody," Jennie coaxed. "Let's go." Jennie put her hands by Karen's on the rope and tugged gently. After giving a delicate snort, Dody allowed herself to be led over to the fence, where the girls tied the goat's rope in a double knot. In a minute Colleen and the others were back with handfuls of grass, which Dody immediately began munching.

"I hope she'll stay put," Karen said nervously. The bell rang, and the girls rushed to line up at the back door of the school.

"She'll be fine," Jennie said. "She's tied up and has grass to eat. Besides, we'll be dismissed in less than an hour."

Karen cast a last worried glance at her goat as the girls marched into school. "I hope so."

Mrs. Hoffman tried to calm down everyone, but for once the class couldn't seem to concentrate as their teacher read *Tom Sawyer* to the class. The students wiggled, whispered, and strained to look out the window at Dody, who was just out of sight around a corner. When the principal appeared in their doorway and asked Mrs. Hoffman to come to his office, she threw up her hands and told the students to leave, even if it was ten minutes early.

Jennie stopped at the water fountain for a drink, which made her almost the last person out the back door. By the time she reached the playground, a big commotion was coming from near the Boy Scout float.

"That goat is eating our float!"

"Stop her, someone!"

"Grab her rope!"

The boys yelled, and the girls laughed. Dody stood calmly in the middle of the turmoil, chewing on a tin can she had pulled off the float.

Jennie couldn't keep from laughing, too. Karen's grandmother had said that goats would eat anything, but Jennie hadn't thought that meant tin cans, too.

"What are you laughing about?" Tommy asked. He planted himself in front of his sister, his hands on his hips. "That animal is destroying our float."

Jennie laughed some more. "You've got to admit that it's pretty funny. A tin can, for Pete's sake."

"Stop her!" Tommy yelled.

"Oh, all right," Jennie said. "Dody can't hurt that float," she muttered as she joined Karen in grabbing the goat's neck.

"What happened to her rope?" Jennie looked around.

"I think this is all that's left." Karen held up a frayed scrap of rope. "I guess she ate all her grass and then the rope."

"I guess." Jennie grinned. "We've got to have some kind of rope." She looked around again. There were only angry boys and snickering girls. "Here, Colleen, help Karen hold onto Dody. I'll run inside and see if Mrs. Hoffman has any rope in the closet."

"Hurry up," Tommy ordered.

Jennie did hurry. The other classes had emptied out, too, so the halls were quiet. Just as she dashed around the corner, she heard an odd noise. She stopped and listened, forgetting her mission. It came from her classroom, where the door stood partway open. She walked quietly up and peeked in the door. Mrs. Hoffman sat at her desk with her head down. The noise was the muffled sound of her crying.

Jennie backed up as a chill raced through her. She wasn't sure what to do. She didn't want to bother Mrs. Hoffman, but should Jennie help? What was wrong? She retreated into the hall as she tried to decide.

At the sound of foodsteps, Jennie swung around to see Tommy.

"Did you get the rope?" he demanded. "That goat got away again."

Jennie put her finger over her lips to hush Tommy. He frowned but obeyed. "What's wrong?" Tommy whispered.

Jennie tiptoed over to the classroom door and motioned. "I don't know if we should go in or not," she whispered.

Tommy peeked in the room and looked back at his sister, eyes wide with concern. They looked at each other for a moment before Jennie said, "Come on. Let's see if we can help."

They entered the classroom, which seemed unfamiliar when filled with the sound of weeping. Slowly they walked to Mrs. Hoffman. "What's wrong? Can we help?" Jennie asked.

Mrs. Hoffman raised a tear-stained face from her arms. Jennie felt like she might cry, too. "What's wrong, Mrs. Hoffman?" Jennie asked again.

The tears ran freely down Mrs. Hoffman's face, but Jennie saw their teacher take a deep breath. "I'm sorry to be crying." She swiped at her face with a hand and sniffed. "It's just that. . ." She hesitated, and the tears poured down her cheeks once again. "It's my husband. He's been shot down. Killed. . ." Sobs shook her shoulders, and she placed her head on her arms once more.

Shock zapped through Jennie. The handsome pilot in the picture gone, just like that? How could that be? Jennie knew men died in the war, lots of men, but surely not the kind of men who took time to write to kids. Not the kind of men who had wives as nice as Mrs. Hoffman.

Shock turned to anger. This wasn't fair. God wasn't fair if He let such things happen. Jennie wanted to shake her fist and yell out her anger. But she didn't. Maybe later she could do that, but now all she could do was stand beside Tommy. Behind them a breeze puffed in through the open windows and fluttered the flags that stuck out of their map. Jennie stared at that map, which would have one less flag and one more cross now. Her eyes prickled, and a tear ran down her cheek.

CHAPTER 8

Birthday Surprises

The parade went on that day, but the sparkle was gone for all the students from Mrs. Hoffman's class. Dody had cooperated as well as a goat could, and the boys had walked beside their float as the motorcycle pulled it slowly down the street. The principal had driven Mrs. Hoffman home after she had hugged Jennie and Tommy and asked them to tell the others. It was a black day for Mrs. Hoffman's fourth-grade class.

But the days of fall went by, and eventually even Mrs. Hoffman's pale face perked up a little. Her students tried their best to behave, and she often told them how much it helped her feel better. Mr. Hoffman's flag on the map was the only one that had been switched to a cross so far that fall. Jennie prayed every day that Roger's wouldn't be next.

The family had received occasional letters from Roger, and they guessed he was still fighting in Italy. The letters had stopped abruptly at the end of October, which made everyone a bit uneasy. The radio announcer said that the fighting in Italy was fiercer and taking much longer than expected, but that the Allies were gaining ground foot by foot.

Mr. Romano still hadn't heard from his brother, and there was no news about Mike Fancher. Jennie had heard her father say that no news was good news. Maybe that was the case with Mike and Roger and Mr. Romano's brother.

Guests moved in and out of the hotel, and always there were a million sheets to change and acres of floors to sweep and mop. Pietro still lived with Mr. Romano, although as far as Jennie could tell, he only ate and slept at his cousin's apartment. Jennie thought the man only lived with Mr. Romano to eat the Italian man's cooking, because Pietro was definitely getting plumper.

Christmas was quiet for everyone. Jennie wondered if the others were remembering last Christmas when people were saying that the war would be over by the next year. Nobody said that now. This was the third Christmas that Roger had been gone, and Mama's face was solemn as the family bundled up to go to church on Christmas Eve.

Jennie planned to pray all the way through the service. She was over being mad at God, but she still didn't understand very much about this war. Mama had said that the Bible tells people to pray without ceasing, so that's what Jennie planned to do.

January started out cold and dreary. The sun didn't peek out for days at a time. Jennie and Tommy plodded through their chores at the hotel, arguing every chance they got. All Jennie wanted was one sunny afternoon when she and Colleen could go down to the waterfront, sit on the wharf, and watch the dockworkers unload ships. But it didn't happen.

Then Trudy caught a bad cold. She was sick for two weeks, and the others had to take over her work. Jennie didn't mind because her sister had done Jennie's work many times, but Jennie missed the only two sunny afternoons. By the time Trudy was better, it was the end of January and the day of Jennie's and Tommy's birthdays. They had been born on the same day one year apart, and they always celebrated together. Jennie was turning ten years old and Tommy would be nine.

"Do you think they've forgotten about our party?" Tommy asked. The pair were on cleanup duty again that Saturday morning. They were supposed to be sweeping the lobby and long hallways.

"Maybe," Jennie said as they dragged the dust mops out of the closet.

"I didn't think Mama would forget." Tommy frowned.

"Me either," Jennie said, "but maybe she'll remember later. Don't say anything for a while. If she still doesn't remember, we'll give her some hints."

"We could do that, couldn't we?" Tommy's face perked up.

"Sure," Jennie said. "Come on, let's try out these new dust mops." She pushed at the long handle that ended with a mop head that looked like a huge gray mustache. "This is just like the janitor uses at school. When I was in first grade, I always wanted to ask him if I could get on the mop head part and ride while he pushed."

"Did you ever ask?"

"No. I was scared to talk to him," Jennie said.

Back and forth across the lobby they went, sweeping the dirt and tiny debris in front of them. The hard part was what to do with the dirt they swept up. Jennie had a feeling they were supposed to get the whisk broom and dustpan, but that was a lot of trouble. Instead, when they were sure no one was watching, they swept it out the front door and down the steps.

Jennie had just given her mop a hard shake outside at the bottom of the steps when a voice spoke up. "Excuse me. Do you know if Mr. Pietro Contadino lives in this hotel?"

Jennie jerked around and in doing so whacked her mop handle against the wall near where Tommy stood with his mop. She flinched at the noise, and Tommy ducked. "Sorry," she muttered to her brother before turning to the owner of the voice.

A young woman stood on the sidewalk. Jennie realized that the woman was pretty, but that wasn't what she noticed most of all. She was dressed in black from head to toe. She wore a long coat with a slouchy kind of hat and odd-looking black boots. A cigarette dangled from her fingertips at the end of a sticklike holder. The only touch of color was her lips, and they were covered with bloodred lipstick.

"Pietro?" Jennie asked.

"Yes, Pietro lives here." Tommy pushed Jennie aside. "His room is at the top of the stairs in the last hallway off the lobby. It's apartment four."

"Thank you." The woman in black made her way up the stairs.

"Interesting," Tommy said.

"I wonder what she wants with Pietro," Jennie mused.

"Just a friend, I suppose." Tommy started up the stairs.

Jennie lifted her eyebrows but didn't say anything. This woman might be one more clue in the mystery of Pietro, or she might be collecting for some charity. If that were the case, she'd be out of luck with Pietro.

Jennie and Tommy carried their mops to the closest hallway.

"Let's get this done. I'm tired of looking at dirt," Tommy said.

Jennie bent over to pick up a piece of paper that lay on the floor near the apartment where Jasper lived with his father. "Look," she said and held it out for Tommy to see. "It's a movie star picture."

"It's Lana Turner," Tommy said after looking at the picture.

"I know," Jennie said. "I wonder how it got in the hall?"

"I think it's Jasper's," Tommy answered. "I've seen it in his school notebook before. Lots of the older boys have pictures of movie stars."

"He should be more careful with it," Jennie said. "She is pretty, but I like Clark Gable better. I saw him on a newsreel last week at the movies."

"I saw Lana Turner on one, too, a couple of weeks ago." Tommy put the picture on a nearby ledge. "She was talking to some soldiers."

"I guess all those movie stars try to help out with the war effort." Jennie sighed. "I wish Clark Gable would help out here."

"Forget movie stars," Tommy said. "We've still got one more hallway to sweep." They carried their mops through the lobby. The last hallway stretched out endlessly before them.

"Let's race," Jennie said. "We'll see who can get their mop to the end of the hall and back first. The sweeping will be done, and we'll know who's the fastest." She gave a wide smile and waited for Tommy to bristle up.

"That won't be any contest," Tommy said quickly.

"We'll just see about that," Jennie said. "Come over here and make a starting line."

"I wish we had someone to say go." Tommy lifted his mop and went over to the end of the hall.

"Well, we don't," Jennie said, "unless you want to ask Mama." Jennie was teasing because their mother was likely to take a dim view of another race.

"I guess that won't be necessary." Tommy stuck out his tongue at his sister.

They lined up and Jennie said, "Ready, set, go!" Off they went, flying down the hallway, with their mops in front. Jennie was a little ahead when they made the turnaround at the end, but she caught her mop for a second on a broken edge of the linoleum, slowing her down. She turned on the speed to catch up and had almost accomplished that when Mrs. Parker opened her door and stepped out into the hall. She was dressed in her good black coat and hat and had her handbag over her arm. Her head was ducked down a little as she tucked something in her pocket.

Jennie saw their neighbor but quickly realized that Tommy didn't. Her brother had turned his head toward her, probably to see how far behind she was. Jennie opened her mouth to yell, but it was too late. Tommy crashed into Mrs. Parker, who saw the boy just in time to avoid being bowled over but not in time to keep her purse from going one direction and her hat the other as she tried to move out of the way. Tommy ended up on the floor with a thud.

Jennie dropped her mop and hurried to help Tommy and get Mrs. Parker's bag and hat. "Are you all right?" Jennie asked the older woman and then her brother.

Tommy nodded and looked nervously at Mrs. Parker, who seemed to be gathering up steam to speak.

"I am just fine, I assure you." The woman yanked her handbag and hat away from Jennie. "No thanks to you two young hooligans."

"We're sorry," Jennie began. "We were sweeping the floor."

"Spare me the details." Mrs. Parker jammed her hat back on her head. "You're both incorrigible, and your mother shall hear about this." She stalked off down the hall, her back stiff and her chin held high.

"What's *incorrigible*?" Jennie asked.

"I don't know, but I don't think it's something that Mama is going to like," Tommy answered. "We'll be in trouble for sure, and on today of all days. This is all your fault. If you hadn't wanted to race, I wouldn't have run into her."

"You should have watched where you were going." Jennie beat a hasty retreat down the hall with her mop.

"Jennie, Tommy, come quick!" Trudy yelled from the hotel lobby.

"That was fast." Jennie frowned. Getting in trouble didn't seem to take any time at all these days. She put away her mop and dashed toward the office, leaving Tommy to catch up. Might as well get this over with. She slowed as she approached the office and put on what she thought of as her sorry face. It couldn't hurt, and she was sorry— even though Mrs. Parker was a grouch sometimes.

"Where's Tommy?" Mama asked. Her eyes sparkled but not with anger. She was excited. Jennie looked around a moment before answering, but Mrs. Parker was nowhere to be seen.

"He's coming," Jennie said. She forgot about looking sorry because apparently she wasn't in trouble yet. "What's going on?"

"Wait for Tommy," her mother said.

Then Jennie saw that she had an envelope in her hand. It looked like the kind of envelope that Roger always used. "Is it a letter from Roger?"

Mama nodded, her smile wide. "Tommy," she called down the hall, "hurry up!"

"Go ahead and open it," Jennie said.

"No, it's addressed to you and Tommy," Mama said. "For your birthdays, I imagine. After no letters for weeks and weeks, your birthday letter manages to get here on the right day. It's God's gift."

Tommy arrived, and they all crowded around to listen as Jennie read Roger's letter aloud. Written on Christmas afternoon, Roger's letter had evidently been missed by the censors because there were no cutouts where words had been removed. He didn't say directly where he was, but he talked about trying Yorkshire pudding and going to church at a big cathedral and about the day after Christmas being called Boxing Day. Mama said it sounded to her like he was in England. She said that other letters written before this one would probably arrive soon, and they might mention that he had moved to a different place.

"England will be safe, won't it?" Jennie asked.

"I should think it would be much safer than Italy," Mama replied, "and much more comfortable, too. There's no ground fighting there."

"Why would he be sent there?" Trudy asked. "They don't use tanks in England."

"I can't answer that," Mama said. "Maybe it's only temporary." Her face sobered for a moment. "But we're not going to think about that now." She smiled at them. "We're going to have a celebration. We've heard from Roger, and it's time for a birthday party."

Jennie and Tommy cheered and danced around their mother.

"Did you think we'd forgotten your birthdays?" Mama asked Jennie later.

"Maybe," Jennie admitted. "We wondered, anyhow."

"I could never forget the day I got the biggest surprise of my life," Mama said, putting her arm on Tommy's shoulders. "Two babies only a year apart."

That evening after Dad came home from Boeing, they all gathered in the apartment living room to celebrate. Mr. Romano and Aunt Irene came, too, and they all ate big bowls of ham and beans with cornbread. Aunt Irene had used her meat points to get a nice chunk of ham, and Mr. Romano had baked the best corn-bread Jennie had ever eaten. After they had finished the beans, Mama disappeared into the kitchen and in a few moments came back triumphantly carrying a big cake.

"It's chocolate," she announced. "We've been saving sugar and cocoa a little at a time for weeks. Happy birthday!"

Jennie felt her mouth water. She missed sweets more than anything else that was in short supply during the war. She thought she could eat this cake all by herself, but of course she wouldn't, since everyone else's mouth was probably watering, too.

They ate cake and talked about Roger's letter, and then, as usual, the talk turned to the war. Jennie felt full and happy as she listened to Dad, Mr. Romano, and Aunt Irene talk about how much longer the war could last. The war was terrible, but sometimes there were happy times, and this night was one of them.

"It turned out to be a great birthday, right, sister?" Tommy asked as he lowered himself to the floor near Jennie. They sat a little apart from the others.

"Sure did," Jennie agreed. "I wasn't too sure it would after this morning."

Tommy frowned. "In all the excitement of the letter, I almost forgot that," he said. "Did Mama say anything to you about the mop problem?"

Jennie shook her head. "No, but maybe she's waiting to punish us until after our birthday is over."

"Or maybe Mrs. Parker didn't tell her."

They looked at each other for a moment. It was another time when they didn't have to talk out loud to know what the other one was thinking.

"Mama says Mrs. Parker has a real sweet tooth," Jennie said.

"There's a piece of cake left," Tommy added. "It was for us to split."

Jennie sighed. "I know." She got up from the floor. Talk and laughter vibrated in the living room as everyone offered opinions on every possible subject. She loved family gatherings. "Come on." Jennie motioned to Tommy.

In a few minutes they were knocking at Mrs. Parker's door. She opened the door and frowned at the pair.

Jennie held out the piece of cake, which they had placed on a plate and carefully covered with a napkin. "This is for you, Mrs. Parker."

"It's from our birthday cake," Tommy added.

"We're really sorry about this morning," Jennie said. "We'll be more careful from now on." She watched the woman's face and saw surprise and something else there.

Slowly Mrs. Parker reached out and took the cake. "Well, I should hope so," she said acidly, but her voice softened when she lifted the napkin and looked at the peace offering. "Oh, I do so love chocolate cake."

"It's delicious," Jennie said.

Tommy nodded. "Our mother is the best cook ever."

A real smile lit up Mrs. Parker's face for the first time that Jennie could remember. She looked much younger and sort of pretty.

"We better go," Tommy said.

"Thank you, children," Mrs. Parker said, "and happy birthday."

Jennie and Tommy tramped back down the hall toward their own apartment where the celebration could still be heard.

"I sure would have liked to eat more cake," Jennie admitted.

"Me, too," Tommy agreed.

"Maybe by this time next year, the war will be over," Jennie said. "And we'll have cake and cookies and pudding and fudge and. . ."

"Steak and licorice and—"

"We don't like licorice," Jennie interrupted.

"We might by then," Tommy said, "so we want there to be plenty."

"You're right," Jennie said. "And peppermints. . ."

"And gasoline and tires so we can go to the country again."

They walked down the hall trying to think up all the things that they might have next year. For once the brother and sister were in perfect agreement.

CHAPTER 9

The Junk Car

At last the long, rainy winter had passed, and May brought a series of sunshiny days perfect for scrap metal prospecting. This year's Victory garden had been planted but didn't need to be weeded yet, so Jennie and Colleen had planned a whole Saturday to look for scrap.

There was to be a big rally on June 12 to celebrate the beginning of the fifth war loan drive, and that same day would be the end of a scrap metal drive that had started last week. Jennie and Colleen planned to show the boys how this collecting business should be done.

"What do you hear from Roger these days?" Colleen asked as the pair started out Saturday morning after chores were finished. The plan was to crisscross the streets and alleys south of Cedar Avenue, looking for metal of any kind. They each carried old burlap bags for their finds.

"We've had lots of letters from him lately," Jennie replied. "I don't think he has much to do in England." She stopped for a moment to peer around a building corner. The alley was bare except for two cats sunning on a stoop.

"Why is he still there?"

Jennie shrugged her shoulders. "Don't know. At least not for sure. Dad says that sooner or later the Allies will invade Europe. He doesn't say it, but I think he wonders if Roger is waiting to do that." Jennie had a feeling that Dad didn't talk much about that because of Mama. She had been so cheerful this winter just knowing that Roger was in England.

The girls walked and talked and looked for close to an hour. Finally Colleen lifted up an old tarp that lay in a corner near the back door of a warehouse. "Nothing here, either. We've been looking forever and don't have a single piece of scrap that amounts to anything." She dumped her sack and a rusted piece of bucket tumbled out.

"You're right," Jennie said. All she had in her sack was a mashed toy car. "We've had so many scrap drives that I guess there's not much left."

"We'll never win the contest at this rate," Colleen said. "What about the boys? Are they collecting today, too?"

"They went with Art back to our old house. Tommy said that Art wanted to get something out of the shed, but I think they're looking for scrap." Jennie leaned over to pick up a long bolt that she saw in the gutter.

"That doesn't seem fair," Colleen said. "It's your house, too."

Jennie grinned. "I checked it out last week when I went with Trudy to collect the rent and get Mama's good tablecloth out of the box in the attic. There's nothing there any better than this junk." She ran into the street to pick up a squashed old teapot.

"I guess it all adds up," Colleen said.

"Yeah, but not fast enough to win that contest. We need something big."

"Like what?" Colleen asked.

"I don't know." Jennie stopped for a moment. "Something like a machine that isn't any good anymore."

"Where would we find that?"

"Not around here. That's for sure," Jennie said. "Maybe we should get on the bus and go farther south, where there are more houses instead of apartments, or even farther where there are factories."

"Couldn't hurt," Colleen said. "We could go out near Boeing. It's not that far, really."

A quick trip back to the hotel got them some lunch and permission from Mama to go if they'd be back before dark. A half hour later they were on the bus headed south.

"I haven't been out here since the plane crash last year," Jennie said. She hadn't thought about that crash in a long time. She wondered again if the woman who had called for Raymond had ever found him.

"Let's get off at the next stop," Jennie said. "We're almost to the Boeing factory. We can circle around and see what we can find."

They pulled the bell and climbed off the bus at the next corner.

"Tell me again what we're looking for," Colleen said after they had walked a block.

"We'll know it when we see it."

Colleen raised her eyebrows. "Maybe you will, but I need a little more to go on."

Jennie laughed. "Come on, let's look over there." She pointed to an overgrown vacant lot across the street. It looked a little like the Victory garden lot before they had plowed it up, but the grass and weeds were much taller. Jennie doubted she and Colleen could see over the tops, even though they were both pretty tall for their age.

"You really want to go in that jungle?" Colleen asked doubtfully. The girls crossed the street and stood at the edge of the lot.

"It doesn't look like anyone else has been in there lately, either," Jennie said. "Who knows what we might find?"

"Snakes and bugs," Colleen muttered.

Jennie waded in the weeds a few feet. "Look here, a bunch of little paths. Probably made by small animals."

"Wild animals! In Seattle?" Colleen stopped abruptly.

"I didn't say wild," Jennie said. "They might be dog trails or rabbit tunnels."

"Oh," Colleen said.

The girls pushed through the tall weeds, following the paths that crossed the big lot. Every so often, Jennie stopped and looked around. Toward the rear of the lot was a stand of brushy trees, and she gradually led the the girls closer to that area.

"What's that big lump over there?" Colleen asked the next time they stopped. She pointed to the right.

Jennie strained her eyes in that direction. There was a big brownish something in the thicket of trees. She pushed closer. "It looks like. . ."

"A junk car," Colleen finished.

Sure enough, the rusting hulk of an old car rose out of the weeds and brush. Silly as it seemed, it looked to Jennie as if it had grown there. The tires had long since flattened into puddles of rotted rubber, and the rust patches made the light brown paint look spotted.

"Wow! This would make a ton of scrap," Jennie said.

"Are you crazy?" Colleen asked. "How could we get this out of here, and who does it belong to anyway?"

"Problems to be solved, that's all." Jennie grinned. "It could be done."

"I guess nobody must want it or it wouldn't be rusting away out here," Colleen said.

"We'd try to find the owner." But Jennie couldn't imagine any owner who wouldn't be glad to get rid of such a big piece of junk.

"How would we get it to the collection center?" Colleen pushed through the brush to look at the front of the old heap. "The boys could never find something this big. We'd be sure to win the contest." Her eyes lit up.

"I was thinking the same thing," Jennie said. "Not that it matters, of course." She peeked inside the broken side window of the car. The backseat's stuffing had been pulled out and scattered. "Looks like some field mice have been living in here. I guess they'll have to move."

"*If* we can figure out how to get this car out of here," Colleen said.

"Oh, we'll think of something. We always do."

The girls backtracked through the weeds to the street and started the trek to the bus stop, talking all the way.

"We'd need some way to pull it out of that lot," Jennie said.

"Once it was out, maybe it could be dragged to the collection center," Colleen said.

"A tow truck is what we need," Jennie said, "but where could we come up with that?"

Colleen stopped short and snapped her fingers. "Stan's father has some kind of a winch on his truck. It's like what they use on tow trucks. I think he just puts it on when he needs to lift or haul something for his job."

"We could ask him if he'd help," Jennie said. "He probably would. He's done lots of war work around the neighborhood."

"Only one problem," Colleen said and started walking again.

"Yeah," Jennie said. "The boys. We'd have to tell them, and we'd have to share the scrap." The girls walked in silence for a few minutes.

"Maybe we could make a deal," Colleen said. "Give them some of the credit, but we get more because we found it."

"Maybe," Jennie said doubtfully. Tommy was way too intent on winning this contest to agree to any kind of deal.

"Look, there's Boeing," Colleen said. The huge factory complex sat off to one side with parking lots around it. "I heard that the roof is camouflaged to look like a little town."

"I couldn't say," Jennie said. The war made lots of talk off-limits, and the fact that the big airplane factory had been disguised to look like a village fell in that category. Sometimes Jennie imagined what would happen if the enemy managed to find out important things about Boeing, like how it was camouflaged or what kind of planes it made. Maybe they'd do something drastic to try to get rid of the factory. That was a scary thought.

"We sure can't see anything from here," Colleen said.

"Too far away from the main buildings," Jennie agreed. They were near the front gate of the complex, which was guarded by several security guards. Outside the gate, men and women milled around, waiting for buses or other rides. Dad said there were always people coming and going because of the different shifts for different production lines.

"Maybe we can catch the bus here," Colleen said.

Jennie nodded. She was tired of walking. They pushed through the crowd until they found a sign for the bus they needed.

"Let's wait right here." Jennie sank down on the street curb.

The girls sat quietly for a few minutes just looking and listening. A couple of buses arrived and departed while Jennie and Colleen watched.

Jennie noticed a familiar figure that stood in a group of uniformed workers across the street. She jabbed Colleen in the ribs. "Look at that! Over there."

"Well, what do you know," Colleen said. "It's good old Pietro."

Sure enough, Mr. Romano's cousin was talking earnestly to a couple of Boeing workers. As the girls watched, Pietro led the pair over to a black car parked on the street nearby. All three climbed into the backseat of the car, but the car didn't pull away.

"What's he doing?" Jennie asked. "He doesn't have a car that I know of. And why isn't he at work at the shipyard?"

"It's not the first time he's skipped work," Colleen said.

"I was up early this morning and saw him leave for work with his lunch pail." Jennie watched as the two Boeing workers climbed out of the car and walked away. In a minute another worker walked up and stuck his head in the open back door of the car, then climbed in and shut the door. What was Pietro up to?

Another figure approached the car but didn't open the door. It was the woman Jennie had seen before, the one dressed in black who had asked for Pietro at the hotel. This time she still wore black but without the long coat and hat. A cigarette dangled once more from a holder she grasped loosely between her fingers, and she leaned against the car's fender.

"Is she with Pietro?" Colleen leaned over to talk in Jennie's ear.

"I've seen her before." Jennie told Colleen about the woman

coming to the hotel looking for Pietro.

As they watched, the worker climbed out of the backseat, followed by Pietro. The woman in black walked over to Pietro, who opened the front car door for her. She slid in, and Pietro started around the car. Just then another man in a Boeing uniform stopped him.

About the same time the bus pulled up at the stop. With a last glance at Mr. Romano's cousin, Jennie and Colleen climbed aboard.

"Quick," Jennie said. "Get that seat over there." She pointed to an empty seat halfway back on the bus. They tumbled into their place and scrambled to stick their heads out the window. Pietro was still talking to the worker. As the bus slowly pulled away from the curb, Jennie saw the man shove something into Pietro's hand and receive some kind of paper in return. Someone shouted from behind Jennie and Colleen on the bus. Pietro's head jerked up at the sound, and in the next instant he looked straight at the bus.

"Duck!" Jennie yelled, and the girls fell back to the seat and stared at each other.

"Do you think he saw us?" Jennie asked. In a moment she sat up enough to peek out the window again as the bus picked up speed. "He's still looking."

"I don't think so," Colleen said. "I think he was looking at the back. What was that all about?"

"I don't know for sure," Jennie answered. There was just so much about Pietro that didn't make sense. What was he doing with the Boeing workers, and why was that woman with him? Jennie frowned as she remembered the paper that had changed hands, the paper that looked like a folded envelope. What could a Boeing worker be giving to Pietro?

There were so many questions and no answers. At the back of Jennie's mind, a prickly thought kept coming back. What if the Boeing workers were giving Pietro information about the factory? Was it possible that Mr. Romano's cousin was a spy?

CHAPTER 10

More Clues

Jennie and Colleen had a lot to mull over for the next week or so. They traipsed through neighborhood after neighborhood, looking for scrap that would be easier to retrieve than the old car. It seemed there wasn't any decent scrap metal left anywhere in Seattle. The other Girl Scouts complained of the same problem and said they were going to collect newspapers instead. Jennie and Colleen weren't ready to give up yet, especially when Tommy and Stan gave no sign of quitting.

Jennie couldn't stop thinking about Pietro, the woman in black, and the Boeing workers. Jennie wanted to go right up to Pietro and ask him what he had been doing at the Boeing gate, but she was sure that wasn't the way to approach a spy. Jennie had decided that the facts pointed in that direction. No, a better plan would be to do a little spying herself with Pietro as the object. To do that she needed to talk to Mr. Romano alone.

"If it isn't my good friend Jennie." Mr. Romano smiled when he opened his front door the following Friday. "Come in and have a piece of biscotti. It's freshly baked."

"Sounds great." Jennie sat down at Mr. Romano's tiny kitchen table.

"I haven't seen you for a week or more." Mr. Romano placed a plate of biscotti in front of Jennie. "You've been a busy girl."

Jennie nodded and chewed her cookie. Mr. Romano pulled a milk bottle out of the small refrigerator and motioned to it. Jennie nodded again and gratefully accepted a glass of milk. Now that Jennie was here to check up on Pietro, she wasn't sure how to go about it.

"How are you these days?" she asked.

"I'm just fine," Mr. Romano replied. "I love this sunny weather we've been having almost as much as my geraniums do." He nodded his head in the direction of the window where geraniums and other plants stretched toward the afternoon sun.

"Does Pietro like the sunny weather, too?" Jennie asked. It seemed as good a way as any to switch the conversation to the cousin.

"Can't say that Pietro notices things like sunshine all that much," Mr. Romano said. A slight shadow passed over his face at the mention of his cousin. "Besides, he spends most of his time indoors when the sun is out."

"Is he still on the day shift?" Jennie was sure she knew the answer, but a detective should double-check her facts.

"Has been for months now," Mr. Romano replied. "Lately he's been working twelve-hour shifts again."

"Does he work on weekends, too?"

"All the time. I think most shipyard workers do," Mr. Romano said. "Say, you're quite interested in old Pietro's schedule. Why?"

Jennie shrugged and grinned at her friend. "Just wondering, that's all." She didn't want to say anything to Mr. Romano about Pietro's comings and goings until she knew more facts.

"So tell me about the latest contest with the boys," Mr. Romano said. "Knowing you children as I do, I'm sure there is one."

Jennie took one last drink of milk before telling Mr. Romano about the junk car and her hopes to get it for the scrap drive. The older man listened and nodded once in a while.

"So what do you think?" Jennie asked. "Do you have any ideas about getting that car to the collection center?"

"Sounds to me like you already have a good idea," Mr. Romano said. "Stan's father would be your best bet. I've met him before at Civil Defense meetings. I think he'd help you."

"But then we'd have to let the boys in on the plan and probably have to share the scrap with them, too."

"So you said," Mr. Romano replied, "but maybe it's more important to get all that scrap for the war effort than it is to beat the boys. At least you should think about it."

"I will," Jennie promised as she got up to leave. Getting the old car was one thing, but what about Pietro? Catching a spy would be even more important for the war effort, but Jennie was a long way from having enough information to do that.

Memorial Day was the following Tuesday, and Jennie still didn't know anything more about Pietro by then. Colleen had gone to visit some cousins before they could decide what to do about the car, but she said she'd be back for Tuesday's ceremonies. Then they'd decide what to do.

Tuesday turned out to be yet another sunny day, perfect for the Memorial Day observances that were planned all over Seattle. Jennie dressed carefully in her Girl Scout uniform about noon and went with Tommy, who was in his Boy Scout uniform, to meet the rest of the family in the hotel lobby. Even Dad had a half day off from work. Jasper's dad had volunteered to watch the office so the whole Fleming family could attend. Aunt Irene and Mr. Romano had gone on ahead in Aunt Irene's car to save a place for their picnic.

"Don't you two look official," Dad said. He and Art stood by the office door.

"I get to carry a flag in the procession," Jennie said proudly.

"My troop will be there, too," Tommy said.

"But without flags," Jennie said and saw her brother make a face.

"No arguing from either of you," Mama said as she came out of the office carrying a picnic basket. Behind her, Trudy carried a smaller basket. "This is a day for us to enjoy being together."

"And honor our fighting men and women," Dad added. He took Mama's basket from her, and Art took Trudy's. In a few minutes the family was out the door and squeezing into the DeSoto for the trip to the cemetery.

"Why is the Memorial Day ceremony held at the cemetery?" Tommy asked.

"Yeah," Jennie said, "why is that? A cemetery doesn't seem like the right place for a celebration." She had thought about that last night before she went to sleep. A cemetery was a place of death, but they were going there for a picnic.

"Depends on how you look at it," Dad said over his shoulder as he steered through the traffic. "We're celebrating our country and what it stands for, but we're also honoring the men and women who have died to protect it."

"I have a few flowers to decorate some graves," Mama said.

"I'm just sorry that it's too soon for our Victory garden zinnias to be in bloom."

"But we don't know anyone who is buried in this cemetery," Tommy said.

"It doesn't matter," Mama said. "We'll just decorate some graves that don't have any flowers already."

Jennie leaned back in the seat where she sat wedged in between Art and Tommy. She wondered if Mrs. Hoffman was decorating her husband's grave today. Their teacher had moved the day after school dismissed for the summer. She had gone back to her hometown in Missouri, the place where she had met her husband. Jennie thought about that for a few moments before she remembered that Mrs. Hoffman couldn't decorate her husband's grave. His body hadn't been brought back to the United States.

It didn't take long to get to the cemetery, but they had to park a long way from the platform that had been built for the ceremony.

"Jennie," a voice hollered, "over here!" Colleen waved at Jennie from behind a stone wall that surrounded a group of graves. Jennie hurried over to join the rest of her Girl Scout troop.

"We thought you weren't going to make it," Colleen said. "It's almost time to start."

"We had to wait for Dad," Jennie said. "Where do I stand?"

"Here," Colleen said and handed Jennie a small American flag. "Walk behind me."

A band up ahead began to play, and the girls fell into step. They marched up the center aisle between crowds of people who sat on wooden folding chairs. When they got to the platform, they stopped and lined either side of the stairs. Jennie saw Tommy and Stan with the other Boy Scouts off to one side of the platform, where they stood in salute to the flags.

The dignitaries marched down the aisle and up the steps between Jennie and Colleen and the others. Jennie saw several older men in military uniforms, World War I veterans, she was sure, and two younger uniformed men. One of them was on crutches and slowly made his way up the steps while the other young man walked beside him. The second man's uniform coat sleeve was empty, pinned up so it wouldn't dangle. Both men must be wounded veterans of this war, Roger's war.

Bringing up the rear were a couple of other men in suits. One of them was a minister, who grinned at Jennie before mounting the platform. After all the dignitaries were lined up on the stage, the Girl Scouts filed down to stand in front of chairs on the front row, and the band finished with a flourish.

The ceremony got under way with the Pledge of Allegiance, after which everyone sank into their chairs. There were speeches from the older veterans and speeches from the young ones. Finally the talking was over, and Jennie sat up straighter. It was time for the reading of the roll of honor. That job had been given to the minister.

He read the names of soldiers from Seattle who had been killed in the past year. His deep voice hesitated between each name as if to give that soldier his due. It was a long list, but no one in the audience stirred. At last Jennie heard what she had been waiting for—Mr. Hoffman's name. She had made sure that Mr. Hoffman was on the minister's list.

The last name hung in the air for a moment before the sound of a bugle pierced the silence. Jennie tilted her head to listen. It was coming from a little hill among the gravestones a hundred yards away. Jennie had heard "Taps" played before but never like this. Her heart felt torn apart as she listened to the clear notes of the bugle that surged across the cemetery. It played in honor of Mr. Hoffman and all the others dead in countries far from the one they defended. The bugle seemed to hold all that pain and send it floating out over the crowd. As the last note faded, Jennie heard sniffs and sighs all around her and some quiet sobbing, too.

Then it was over, and everyone began to talk and laugh and look for their picnic baskets. Jennie realized that she was starved, and she and Colleen set off to find their families.

Mama had spread a couple of blankets on the grass near the platform. Many other people had done the same, so there was a big crowd. Colleen's family joined the Flemings, and in a minute Stan and his family came up to spread their blanket next to the others. Aunt Irene and Mr. Romano were already settled and pulling food out of their baskets. It was a great big party, and Jennie feasted happily on fried chicken, potato salad, pickles, and lots of other goodies. She and Colleen had to lie back on the blanket to rest before they could dig into the cake that Colleen's mother had brought.

"Got room for a hungry fellow?" a voice asked from the other side of the blanket. Jennie recognized that voice.

"Sure thing, Pietro," Dad said. "Sit down and dig in." Dad scooted over to make room for the neighbor.

"I thought you had to work," Mr. Romano said to his cousin as he handed him a plate. Pietro took the plate and heaped it with food.

"Got off early for the holiday," Pietro answered around a mouthful of potato salad. "Didn't want to miss the ceremonies honoring our soldiers."

"Likely story," Jennie whispered to Colleen. "He probably didn't want to miss a good meal."

Colleen snickered. "He's not missing anything."

The girls watched as Pietro loaded up his plate a second and then a third time. Jennie shook her head. It was a good thing that Mama had fried that extra chicken and brought more rolls than she had first planned.

"We better get our cake," Colleen said, "or there won't be any left."

After eating, Jennie and Colleen wandered off to look at gravestones and read the inscriptions that were carved on the stones. At first Jennie felt funny walking among the graves, some of which had been carefully decorated with flowers, but soon she and Colleen were going from one to the other to look at the names and dates.

"This man was ninety-five when he died," Jennie said after some quick arithmetic in her head.

"This woman was ninety-nine," Colleen said from in front of a tall stone with flowers carved on the top.

"Women always live longer than men," Jennie said.

"That's not true." Tommy popped out from behind the stone, followed by Stan. "Stan and I will prove it. We'll find two or three men who died when they were a hundred years old or more. You won't find a single woman that old."

"That's where you're wrong," Jennie said. "Come on, Colleen, let's show these boys that women always win."

"Even in the graveyard." Colleen laughed.

The children ran from stone to stone, weaving across the cemetery, careful to avoid the flowers. Calling out dates to each other, they searched for the oldest occupants.

"Here's a woman who was ninety-nine," Colleen called from the front of a huge gravestone.

"So was this man," Stan yelled.

"Doesn't count," Jennie said. "They have to be at least a hundred."

They worked their way farther apart until Jennie ended up alone near a group of identical gravestones. They were much smaller than most of the other stones and worn by age. Curious, she walked closer to read the inscriptions. It was one family. Stone after stone revealed that the children had died within days of each other in 1918. Jennie remembered reading in school about a big flu epidemic that killed thousands of people that year. Two stones at the very end proved to be soldiers who died in World War I about the same time as the children. No doubt they were older brothers.

"What are you looking at?" Colleen asked as she walked up. "Did you find a real old one?"

"No," Jennie said, "just the opposite." She waved to the row of stones. "They all died too young."

Colleen stared at the names and dates. "I see what you mean."

"Why does God do that?" Jennie asked. "Why does He let a whole family die?" She didn't really expect Colleen to have an answer, but she just had to say it out loud. There was so much about life and death that she questioned these days.

"You're asking the wrong person," Colleen said, "because I don't know." She reached down and gently brushed a pile of leaves away from the base of one of the stones. "Why don't you ask God? He's the one in charge and the one with the answers."

"How would He answer?" Jennie asked.

"My mother says that He finds a way," Colleen said, "and I think she's right. Sometimes when I pray about something, like a problem or a choice, the answer will come to me."

"Like magic?" Jennie asked.

"No, it's not like that. It's quieter, and it usually takes longer. Sometimes I'm not even sure if it's God talking to me, but most of the time I can tell, if I'm paying attention."

"I'll try it," Jennie said. And she would, too. She had lots of questions she wanted to ask God.

Voices rang across the graves, angry voices raised in argument. Jennie and Colleen turned at the same time. Not far away stood three figures behind a small square marble building. Jennie strained her eyes and ears in the strangers' direction. She saw a woman and two men, and they weren't strangers after all, at least not all of them.

Jennie had seen the woman twice before with Pietro. She stood with Mr. Romano's cousin and again wore black. Pietro and the other man were arguing, but Jennie couldn't hear any words clearly. The other man was taller than Pietro and quite skinny compared to Pietro's portly build.

With no hesitation, Jennie motioned to Colleen to follow as she circled around to get closer to the trio. Maybe the mystery of Pietro could be solved if Jennie could hear what the two men were arguing about. At least it might be a clue.

It wasn't hard to sneak up on Pietro and the others, because they all were talking at once. Several large gravestones dotted the area near the marble building, so it was just a question of getting from one to the other without being seen. In a matter of moments Jennie and Colleen were close enough to understand the voices.

"If you can't deliver the goods, I'll get someone else," the tall man said. "You're not the only one of your kind in Seattle. That I can say for sure."

"Don't get so excited," Pietro said. "I said I'd deliver, and I will. I've got another contact to make before I can get everything sewed up. My man is on the day shift at Number Two and needs some persuasion."

"Get him on board or get rid of him," the tall man said. "I want to see something concrete by Saturday, no later. I'll be around to visit you then."

"I'm in the underground now," Pietro said. "She'll show you."

"Depend on it," the tall man said and jerked his head at the woman. "Let's go. This place gives me the willies."

Jennie watched as the trio split up. Pietro walked back toward the picnic area, and the other two headed in the opposite direction.

"What were they talking about?" Colleen asked after a moment or two. The girls sank down to sit on the ground at the base of a big stone.

Jennie shook her head. "I'm not sure, but it didn't sound good at all. Was he talking about getting information from someone? They call the Boeing factory Number Two."

"Maybe it was something else."

"Maybe," Jennie agreed, "but what?" She frowned as the men's words ran through her mind again. They had talked about delivering the goods and using persuasion. It had to be spying, didn't it?

"What are you two doing here?" Tommy demanded. "You're supposed to be looking for hundred-year-old women."

Jennie jumped at her brother's voice. She had totally forgotten their interrupted search.

"We got sidetracked," Colleen said.

"Yeah, that's right," Jennie agreed.

"Was that Pietro I saw walking back toward the picnic area?" Tommy asked.

Jennie nodded.

"What's he doing out here?"

"I don't know," Jennie said. She gave Colleen a warning look. She didn't want to tell Tommy about Pietro and everything that they had heard. Tommy would want to take over and tell Jennie just what to do. She wasn't sure what to do next, but she knew she didn't need her brother to boss her around.

"So did you find any hundred-year-old women?" Tommy asked.

Colleen and Jennie began a good-natured argument about the search, but Jennie couldn't take her mind off Pietro. The tall man had said he'd be back on Saturday. If what Jennie heard was really what she thought she'd heard, there were only four days before Pietro was going to deliver some valuable information about Boeing. Only four days to catch a spy!

CHAPTER 11

The Spy's Lair

"Jennie, what in the world is the matter with you?" Mama asked on Friday afternoon. "You're not my cheerful girl this week. In fact, you've been downright grouchy. Is something wrong?" Mama was sorting sheets in the laundry room while Jennie stacked towels on the shelves.

"Not exactly," Jennie replied. "I'm fine." She smiled as big as she could at her mother. Jennie knew she had been touchy ever since Tuesday.

"Well, if you can't tell me about it," Mama said, "be sure to tell God. He can help."

Jennie nodded and grabbed more towels to stack. She had been telling God, begging Him, in fact, to show her what to do about Pietro. But so far God hadn't answered.

Jennie and Colleen hadn't been able to find out a thing about Pietro all week. Jennie had gotten up early and gone to bed late trying to keep an eye on Pietro but with no luck. The man slipped in and out of the hotel like a ghost. Tomorrow was the deadline the tall man from the cemetery had set, and the girls weren't any closer to catching Pietro. It was enough to make anyone grouchy.

At last the hotel chores were done, and Jennie waited for Colleen in the lobby. It was time for a new plan. Jennie wished she had one to offer.

"I thought we'd be able to follow him," Jennie said a few minutes after Colleen arrived. They sat down on the old couch in the lobby. "We'd follow him and see where his place is, the one he said was in the underground. Once we could prove what he's doing, we'd report him to the authorities."

"Do you think that's where his spy stuff is?" Colleen asked.

"It must be. There isn't room in Mr. Romano's apartment for anything like that."

"What do spies have anyhow?"

"Probably radio equipment," Jennie said, "and maybe files or notebooks."

"Why doesn't he live there? Why does he bother coming back to the hotel every day?" Colleen asked.

"It's his cover," Jennie said firmly. "Who'd suspect a chubby Italian shipyard worker of being a spy? Especially one who comes home for supper every night."

"You're right," Colleen said. "Say, do you think he's spying for the Italians, for Mussolini?"

"Probably," Jennie answered. "Everyone around Seattle is always talking about Japanese spies. That's partly why they sent the Tanakas off to that camp. But unlike the Japanese, an Italian doesn't look any different from other white people, so that makes Pietro a perfect spy."

"Pietro a spy! What are you talking about?" Tommy asked.

"Tommy! What are you doing sneaking up on us and eavesdropping?" Jennie demanded.

"I didn't sneak," Tommy said indignantly. "I walked right up to you, and you weren't talking low or anything."

"Anyhow, it's a private conversation." Jennie turned as if to dismiss her brother.

Tommy ignored her action and planted himself in front of the two girls. "Why do you think Pietro is a spy? That sounds kind of crazy."

"We have our reasons," Jennie replied. She didn't want to tell Tommy about everything. The time for that would be after she and Colleen had caught Pietro in the act.

"He's not a very friendly guy," Tommy conceded. "Most of the time he comes and goes by the fire escape door so he won't have to talk to anyone, but that doesn't make him a spy. You two are nuts."

Jennie gave Colleen a quick look. Pietro came and went by the fire escape door. That would explain why they could never catch him going through the lobby. Colleen grinned a little, and Jennie knew that she had caught on, too.

"You're right," Jennie said, "we're nuts." She felt like shouting now that they had something to go on, a clue Tommy gave, but she still didn't intend to spill the beans to her brother.

Stan came through the hotel front door, and Tommy ran over to him. "You won't believe this," Tommy said. "The girls think Pietro is a spy."

"Let's get out of here before they start asking more questions," Jennie said. The two girls slipped away and down the hall toward Mr. Romano's apartment.

"Why didn't we think of the fire escape?" Colleen asked. They stopped in front of the door in question.

"We would have eventually," Jennie said. She opened the door and looked down at the metal stairs that led to the alley. Pietro could come and go all he pleased and not be noticed.

"Maybe not in time," Colleen said. "Tommy might have other ideas. Don't you think we should ask him and Stan, too?" She peered over Jennie's shoulder at the stairs.

"No," Jennie answered, "we don't need their help. After all, it was just an accident that Tommy mentioned the fire escape. He didn't even know that it was important."

"What's next?" Colleen asked.

"We have to follow Pietro." Jennie shut the fire escape door. "He should be home from work early for supper. I heard Mr. Romano say that Pietro was working a shorter shift this week because of supply problems, and we know he never misses a meal. After that he must go to his place in the underground. We'll be watching the fire escape. From there we trail him and see what we can see."

The girls made their plans and went off to set them in motion. They borrowed Art's flashlight, and a couple of hours later hid behind the trash cans in the alley and waited. Right on schedule, Pietro came walking down the alley, climbed the fire escape stairs, and disappeared inside. A half an hour later he reappeared, still dressed in his work clothes, carrying something wrapped in a white towel.

The girls waited until Pietro was almost out of sight before they followed him. They already knew he would head toward the underground. As soon as they could get lost in the people on the sidewalks, they closed the gap between themselves and Pietro. It wasn't far to the downtown area where the long, hidden, underground passages snaked beneath the streets. Jennie knew many vacant buildings were among the businesses near the waterfront. She guessed that Pietro had his operation set up below street level in one of the abandoned buildings that opened onto the lower, underground level. It would be a perfect place for a spy.

The girls kept close to the buildings they passed just in case Pietro turned around for any reason and they should need to duck inside. The businesses down here weren't ordinary grocery and clothing and hardware stores. Jennie knew that this part of Seattle was the rougher part of town with people and establishments to match. Even so, no one bothered the girls as they made their way closer to the waterfront.

First Pietro was in plain sight, and then he wasn't. Jennie and Colleen looked at each other and all around. Cautiously they approached the spot where they had last seen him, but there was no sign of the man.

"Where did he go?" Colleen said in Jennie's ear.

"He's done his disappearing act again." Jennie scanned the street and sidewalks, looking for any clue. She turned to the nearest building, peering in the window of a door that opened onto the street.

"See anything?" Colleen crowded behind Jennie.

"Maybe." Jennie opened the door. "Look," she said triumphantly. She pointed at a rickety wooden staircase that led down. "He must have gone down here."

Colleen looked down the stairs. "It's dark."

"There's some light," Jennie said. "It must come from other openings like this one."

"Looks pretty dark to me," Colleen said.

"Your eyes will get used to it. Come on, we're going to lose him." Jennie started down the staircase.

The two girls found themselves in an area that looked and felt like a cave. Jennie sniffed at the musty-smelling air. There was a walkway of sorts that led off in the distance to another staircase. A wooden railing that had fallen down in places outlined the walkway, and dusty debris cluttered the sides of the walkway. Using the flashlight, Jennie saw broken furniture scattered across the ground. Boards and piles of bricks were everywhere. Doors and windows were on one side of the underground passage. It looked odd to see them, but Jennie realized that they opened onto a lower level of the existing buildings. She knew from the stories she had heard that the city had rebuilt the streets in this part of town after a fire many years ago. It was perfect for a spy's lair.

Jennie led the way as quickly and quietly as possible. They had already lost valuable minutes when Pietro might even have climbed back up another of the staircases. Jennie strained her eyes. Then she saw a tiny flutter of white. It had to be the towel that Pietro had wrapped around whatever he was carrying when he left the hotel.

"There he is." Jennie pointed.

"Let's get him," Colleen whispered back. The girls hurried along the walkway, following the occasional glimpse of white ahead of them. It wasn't totally silent down here as it might be in a real cave. Jennie could hear traffic noises overhead and occasionally voices. She was thankful for that because it kept this tomb-like place from being quite as scary, and it helped mask any sound the girls might make as they chased Pietro.

After what must have been a couple of blocks at least, a thud sounded up ahead. "He's gone in through a doorway," Jennie said.

"Which one?" Colleen craned her neck to look.

"It has to be this one," Jennie said as they came opposite a big wooden door. The walkway railing in front of that building had been pushed down, and the debris showed dim footprints where someone had walked up to the old door more than once.

"Why didn't he use these stairs?" Colleen waved at the staircase a few steps away. Light from the opening filtered down and offered a fairly clear view of the area near the door and the stairs.

"He didn't want anyone to trace him to this particular spot." Jennie walked over to the door.

"Smart guy," Colleen said.

"Not so smart," Jennie said. "Because we're going to catch him." She tried the knob on the door, but it didn't move. "He locked it."

"Not good," Colleen said. "Is there another way to get in?"

The girls backed up a step or two to look at the front of the underground building.

"Is that a window over there?" Colleen asked.

Jennie looked where her friend pointed. A tiny opening was almost hidden under a beam that supported the sidewalk above. "Good eyes, Colleen. Let's see if we can get in."

The window was small, but the wooden shutter that had covered it drooped from the sash. Jennie pulled the shutter, and it fell to the ground. The window was only a few feet off the ground, so she stuck the flashlight in and looked around. She saw an entryway cluttered with broken chairs and an old table.

Jennie pulled her head back out. "He went in this way. I'd bet on it." Jennie frowned at the window. It was so small. "Let's see if we can make this opening bigger."

They clawed at the frame around the window and managed to break off a piece or two. "Now let me try it," Jennie said. She stuck her head in again and tried to wiggle her shoulders through the opening. "Push!"

Colleen pushed, but Jennie's shoulders just rammed painfully into what was left of the window frame. "Wait!" She pulled back and rubbed her shoulders. "It's still too small."

"Maybe I can make it." Colleen stuck her head in. "Sorry," she said. "Won't work."

"There must be a way to make this bigger." Jennie pulled some more at the window, but the old building was brick and wouldn't give another inch. At last she stopped to rub her scraped knuckles.

"What now?" Colleen asked as they both stood, staring at the window.

"I don't know." Jennie fought the frustration that welled up inside. They were so close, and time was running out. In hours it would be Saturday, the day that Pietro was to have the goods. After that, if Pietro really was a spy, time might run out for other people—people like Dad who worked so hard making the airplanes that helped Roger and the other soldiers fight the war.

A loud sneeze interrupted Jennie's thoughts with a jolt. She whipped around. What now? Had someone caught them spying as they tried to catch a spy themselves? She could see nothing in the dim passageway behind them. Then it came again, sneezing, only this time there were two sneezes in quick succession. They came from near the stairs.

"Who's there?" Jennie called out boldly. She wasn't feeling quite as brave as she made her voice sound, and she could tell by Colleen's face that she was scared, too.

There was no answer, but another sneeze burst out of the darkness. Jennie frowned. Something about that sneeze was familiar, but she couldn't quite think what. It was enough to give her courage, and she walked quickly across the dusty debris to the stairs.

"I said, 'Who's there?' "

Four eyes stared back at her.

CHAPTER 12

Time Runs Out

"Hi," Tommy said weakly and raised his hand in greeting. The other two eyes belonged to Stan.

"What are you doing here?" Jennie demanded.

"I might ask you the same thing." Tommy walked out from behind the stairs. "Does Mama know you're off down here in the underground?"

"Does she know where you are?"

The siblings glared at each other for a moment before Stan spoke. "Knock it off, you two. None of us should be down here. But we are, so out with the story, Jennie."

Jennie wasn't used to Stan being so forceful. It took her by surprise, and she blurted out, "We're following Pietro."

"That's pretty clear," Tommy said. "We saw you follow him from the hotel. That's why we followed you. But why? Does this have something to do with that spy idea of yours?"

"It's not just a crazy idea. We've got to stop him before tomorrow," Jennie said.

"Stop him from what?" Tommy asked.

"It's nothing you need to know about."

Jennie expected Tommy to blow up, but he didn't. Instead he looked thoughtfully at the window behind the girls. "So you want

122

to get inside that window?"

Jennie nodded. "To unlock the door. That's why you two better get out of here and let us get back to work."

"I don't think so." Tommy grinned. "I think you need us."

"What are you talking about?" Colleen asked.

"I can get through that window and open the door." Tommy walked over to the small opening.

"No, you can't," Jennie said. Even as she said it, she knew that Tommy was the smallest and he could probably squirm right through that opening.

"Sure I can." Tommy grabbed a discarded wooden box that was nearby, climbed up on it, and stuck the whole top part of his body through the window.

"Fine," Jennie said impatiently. "Get in there and unlock the door."

"Not so fast." Tommy tapped his fingers on his chin. "First you have to promise you'll tell us what you know about Pietro and this spy business."

Jennie started to protest.

"And," Tommy continued, "you have to let us go along."

"That's no fair," Jennie said. "We want to do this by ourselves."

"Take it or leave it," Tommy said and waited.

"Jennie," Colleen grabbed her friend's arm to pull her aside. "This is no time to work alone just to beat the boys. He's right. We need him, and who knows, we may need both of them before this is over."

Jennie frowned at her friend for a moment, but she knew Colleen was right. What was Jennie thinking? This was about more than beating Tommy at one of their silly contests. Lives might be at stake. They'd have to work together to stop Pietro.

"Get in there," Jennie said. "We don't have a lot of time."

Tommy grinned and nodded at his sister. "I need some help. I'm not going headfirst through that window. Help me get my feet through first."

Colleen and Jennie held up Tommy by the arms while he stuck his feet through the window. With a wiggle or two, the rest of his body followed, and he disappeared inside the building with the flashlight they handed him through the opening. In moments they heard him at the big door, where he threw a bolt and pushed open the door.

"So tell us," Tommy said as he stepped into the passageway. "And make it snappy." Dirt was smeared across his face and down his shirt.

Jennie gave the boys a quick rundown of events, with Colleen adding a detail here and there. "And the tall man said tomorrow was the day," Jennie said. "The day that Pietro has to deliver the goods."

Tommy's eyes seemed to grow bigger. "So you're not crazy. He is a spy. Why are we standing here? There's work to be done, spy-catching work."

Jennie scanned the entryway with the flashlight. It was small and led to a large room on one side and a staircase on the other. Everything was dark and quiet in the large room, so they started up the stairs. Cobwebs brushed Jennie's face once, but she pushed them away and kept going. At the top of the stairs was a long hall-way with many doors. The stairs were in the middle of the hall.

"Which way?" Colleen asked from behind Jennie, who was in the lead.

Jennie listened for a moment, but all she could hear was the distant sound of car horns honking on the street. Which way led to Pietro's hideout? She leaned down to shine the flashlight on the floor. Footprints in the thick dust led off to the right, while in the other direction, the dust was smooth.

"This way," she whispered and turned to the right, moving cautiously down the hall. As each door loomed in front of them, they stopped and listened. Each time Jennie shook her head as they heard nothing and walked on. Once Tommy cautiously opened one of the doors to find a jumble of old furniture and junk.

At last the hallway turned, and all four peeked around the corner before proceeding. There was light up ahead. Jennie guessed it was the late afternoon sun shining in through big windows. They pressed themselves close against the side of the hall and moved toward the light. Jennie heard a rhythmic thudding, faint at first, but growing louder as they went forward. It was an odd sound. She could tell by their faces that the others were mystified, as well.

What could a spy do that would cause a sound like that? Jennie and the others found themselves at the edge of a huge lobby with doorways all around. There was no sign of Pietro or anyone else. The lobby floor was littered with trash. The thudding sound was quite loud now, but it didn't come from the lobby. It seemed to come from above a grand open staircase that rose in the center of the lobby. The railings were carved wood and bordered wide steps. Jennie looked up. The staircase split in two about halfway up. Each narrower staircase curved outward and led to another floor.

Jennie was distracted for just a moment by the grandeur she saw. What a sight this room must have been in the old days. A shove from Tommy brought her back to the present. The odd sound still throbbed and thumped. It definitely came from above. She jerked her head in that direction and started up the stairs. The others followed without a word.

She hesitated a moment at the split in the stairway and turned right. The sound had grown louder. At the top of the stairs was yet another hallway, but this time light from an open doorway lit the way. The rhythmic sound pulsed from the room, and now she could hear another background sound that might be a motor. What was going on?

The four friends circled the pool of light that poured out into the dark hallway and tiptoed up to stand against the wall by the open door. Just as Jennie was ready to peek around the door's edge, the thudding sound stopped. A few seconds later the motor stopped, too. All was silent. Jennie's heart pounded until she thought whoever was inside that room could surely hear it.

They waited, pressed against the wall, listening. A voice said something from a distance. Jennie couldn't make out what was said, but she breathed once again. The voice was nowhere near. Then she heard another voice, equally distant. She listened for a moment and steeled herself to lean out for a quick look.

The room was almost as large as the Flemings' whole apartment and was lit by several lanterns. There were no windows. A row of boxes was stacked across one end of the room. On the far side of the room were some tables with more boxes. Jennie didn't see any radio equipment, but she did see Pietro. The chubby man stood near another man who Jennie didn't recognize. That man sat bent over at one of the tables. Two lanterns glowed on either side of him. It looked like he was writing or drawing, but Jennie couldn't tell for sure.

"It's not good enough," Pietro said loudly. "You'll have to do better than that. Look at this batch. I'm not paying you until you get it right."

Jennie retreated. What was Pietro talking about? Was this the man from Number Two, the one Pietro had mentioned persuading? Jennie leaned around the door again. Pietro was eating something. Occasionally he wiped his hands on a white cloth. It was the towel that had led them to the door in the passageway. Pietro was eating while he betrayed his country. Anger flooded over Jennie. She wanted to get this guy. She motioned for the others to step back.

They held a whispered conference.

"We have to try to get closer," Jennie said. "I can't see enough from here to tell what he's doing."

"Let's go inside then," Tommy said. "We'll sneak behind those boxes you saw."

"It's risky," Jennie said.

Tommy shrugged. "We can't let Pietro get away with this, but we have to have some kind of proof, at least a closer look at what they're doing."

Jennie sighed. Tommy was right as usual. "We'll have to be quiet as mice. If they turn that machine back on, whatever it was, that will help, but we can't be sure they'll turn it back on."

One by one, the four friends slipped into the room and crouched behind the boxes. Jennie led the way as they moved a foot at a time closer to Pietro and the other man. The row of boxes led very close to the table where the man still sat.

"I'm going to give this plate another try," Pietro said. "It still might work, but you keep going on that one."

In a moment a motor *put-putted* to life, and a few seconds later the thudding sound filled the room again. It sounded like something hitting something else, not hard, but hitting nonetheless. Jennie looked at Tommy and the others as they crouched behind the boxes. She was sure now about the motor, but what was that other noise?

Stan sat up straighter and tilted his head. In the dim light, Jennie saw his face tense as he listened. Suddenly he smiled and nodded to himself. He motioned for the others to put their heads close. "It's a printing press," he said.

A printing press! Jennie sat back on her heels. What was a spy doing with a printing press? It didn't make sense. She put her mouth up to Stan's ear. "Are you sure?"

Stan nodded firmly. "One of my uncles had a print shop before the war. That's what a printing press sounds like. I was just too scared to recognize it before."

The noise continued to thud. Jennie raised up enough to peek over the top of the boxes. Pietro stood over a machine that Jennie hadn't noticed before. A printing press, no doubt.

The foursome edged closer to the far end of the boxes, which were barely stacked taller than the children's heads as they crawled. The noisy press covered any sounds the children made. At last they stopped. Any further advance would have to be across the open floor, an open floor that was littered with pieces of paper. Jennie studied the litter that covered the floor. What was that? Several pieces lay just out of her reach. She peeked around the edge of the last box and waited until she saw Pietro turn away. Quickly she leaned out to grab one of the crumpled slips of paper.

The press continued to pound as she crouched back down behind the boxes and smoothed the paper while the others watched. It was printed with red ink and looked familiar, although the printing was too blurred to be read easily.

Tommy grabbed the paper. "It's the front of a ration coupon book." He handed it to Stan.

"But why would he print. . . ," Jennie began. She looked at Tommy, and he slowly nodded. "He's not a spy, he's a counterfeiter," Jennie said.

"He's making ration books to sell on the black market," Tommy said.

"That's almost as bad as being a spy," Colleen said. Though her words were said in a low voice, they suddenly seemed loud because the press stopped just as she said them. Colleen's voice pierced the silence like an arrow.

"Who's that?" Pietro shouted. "I heard someone, Henry. Quick, look over there." Pietro stumbled over a chair as he lurched toward the boxes.

"Run!" Jennie yelled.

Jennie pulled at Tommy's arm while Colleen and Stan scrambled to flee. In a flash the four were around the boxes and out the door. They pounded down the stairs.

"Hey, you kids! Stop right now!" Pietro yelled, but Jennie heard him puffing as he ran.

As Jennie reached the bottom of the stairs, she glanced back. Pietro was behind them, but there was no sign of the other man, the one Pietro called Henry. The big lobby was almost dark now, the setting sun leaving only a glow in the west. It would be even darker in the hallway because Jennie had dropped the flashlight in her haste to run. At least Pietro wouldn't have a light, either.

Pietro had fallen behind on the stairs. Jennie could hear him muttering as he stopped to rest for a moment. Too many rich meals had made Pietro too plump for his own good. That was a lucky break.

The four friends ran down the middle of the dark hallway and reached the top of the last set of stairs. Jennie saw Tommy fling open a nearby door. What was he doing? This was no time to be sightseeing. He dragged something out of the room and put it at the top of the stairs. It was a bench of some sort.

"That'll fix him," he said.

Jennie grabbed his arm again as they climbed over the bench and felt their way down the dark stairs. They smelled the damp air of the underground passage. But now that odor meant escape. Again they felt their way across the entryway of the building and stumbled out into the passageway. A single beam of light shone from near the staircase where Tommy and Stan had hidden earlier. There must be a streetlight right above. Or maybe God had sent a light to guide them. Jennie looked at the beam. Whatever the source, the beam would steer them out of the darkness that pressed all around.

Before they could move, there was a loud clattering behind them followed by an equally loud string of words, all courtesy of Pietro. Tommy chuckled. Their would-be spy had found the bench Tommy had moved. If the anger in Pietro's voice was any guide, he wasn't seriously hurt, but his accident with the bench bought them time.

Colleen led the way, and the other three followed as they climbed the stairs. Fresh air had never smelled so good to Jennie. They ran down the street a little way before stopping near a brightly lit corner.

"I can't believe Pietro is a counterfeiter," Colleen said.

"Instead of a spy." Tommy grinned at his sister.

"The pieces all fit," Jennie said. "I just had the wrong puzzle."

"I would have thought the same thing," Tommy said.

"But how are we going to blow the whistle on him?" Colleen

said. "Will anyone believe us? It is a pretty crazy story."

"Oh, they'll believe us," Stan said. "We have proof."

The other three looked at him, puzzled, until he pulled a piece of paper out of his pocket. It was the crumpled front of the counterfeit ration book that they had looked at earlier.

They cheered before turning toward home and the long explanations that would follow.

CHAPTER 13

Winners

For the next few days, the hotel buzzed with the news of Pietro's counterfeiting. Everyone had an opinion and wasn't afraid to express it. Mr. Romano was very upset by his relative's crime and the opinion toward Italian-Americans. Jennie was glad to see that almost every person in the hotel made a point to tell Mr. Romano that they knew it was no reflection on him that he had a crook for a cousin.

Pietro had disappeared once more, but the police had confiscated his printing press and said they had several leads on finding him. The tall man and the woman in black had been brought in for questioning about a big black-market ring that was operating in the Seattle area. They had been picked up Saturday as they tried to enter Pietro's hideout.

Pietro had been working the black market for months, illegally selling ration coupons, which he stole or bought at a low price. He had been trying to set up his counterfeit operation for some time but lacked a good engraver to make the metal plates for printing the coupons. The man he called Henry had been his latest employee. Henry was nowhere to be found, either.

Jennie realized that Pietro hadn't been interested in Boeing so he could pass information to the enemy; it was just a coincidence that he'd been hanging around the airplane factory while he figured out how to establish his racket.

It was an exciting time for Jennie and Tommy. Mama took turns scolding them for trying to catch a spy and praising them for working together at last. Jennie had to take a little teasing over the spy thing, especially from Art. It helped that Tommy didn't rub in that she had mistaken a counterfeiter for a spy.

The first week of June had been one to remember. The following Tuesday, Jennie was thinking about everything that had happened as she walked home from the Victory garden. It was her day to pull weeds and carry some water to the tomatoes if they needed it. She was also thinking about the scrap drive that she and Colleen still hoped to win, along with Stan and Tommy.

It hadn't really been hard at all to ask the boys to share the scrap from the car. Stan's father was helping them work out all the details before he hauled the junk car to the collecting station. It was no longer girls against boys. Catching Pietro had taught Jennie that working together gets the job done better. Not that she intended to tell Tommy that anytime soon.

There was a stir in the barbershop as she neared the corner. Several people were talking at once. Someone ran out of the barbershop and yelled to no one in particular, "It's started!" Jennie slowed her walk and looked in the window. Five men and a woman stood bunched up near the counter, and others hurried in from the street. What was happening?

The crackling of radio static filled the air briefly. The barber had his radio on the counter with the volume turned up. The people inside the shop quieted. Jennie hurried inside with the others. An announcer came on and said that in a few moments, his station would broadcast a live announcement by an army public information officer. More static followed, and then a steady voice said, "Under the command of General Eisenhower, Allied naval forces supported by strong air forces began landing Allied armies this morning on the northern coast of France." A cheer rose in the barbershop.

Jennie backed away and ran out the door. She wanted to get home and tell her family. The invasion of Europe had begun!

The mood in the hotel varied from jubilation that the war might soon be over to fear for the soldiers who had undertaken such a task. Mama's face paled when she heard the news. Jennie saw Mama close her eyes for a few seconds, and Jennie knew Mama was praying for Roger and the others. But then Mama opened her eyes and smiled, ready to share in the excitement.

There was no news about Roger's part in the invasion, if indeed he had been one of the soldiers splashing ashore on the beaches of France. A few hours later, Jennie and Tommy and the others listened as the famous war correspondent, Edward R. Murrow, reported from London. He said that the bombers going out made the sound of a giant factory in the sky.

Dad said that this was another time when no news was probably good news when it came to Roger. Jennie's spirits rose a little higher each day that passed without a telegram.

At last it was the day of the war bond rally. Stan's father had towed the old car to the collection center, and the four friends had made sure that the weight was carefully recorded so they would get proper credit. The winner of the scrap-collecting contest was to be announced at the rally.

"Hurry up," Jennie said to Tommy. The rally was due to start in an hour, and Tommy was still finishing his chores. For once Jennie had beaten her brother, and she hadn't even been trying.

"There, I'm done." Tommy shoved his dust mop back in the closet. "I'll just wash my hands, and we can go." He ran down the hall toward their apartment.

Jennie groaned. She and Tommy were supposed to meet Colleen and Stan at Victory Square in ten minutes. It wasn't far, but Jennie didn't want to be late.

"Why the rush?" Tommy asked a few minutes later as Jennie hurried him toward downtown. "They won't announce the winner right away. There are always speeches. You know that."

"I heard there might be famous people there," Jennie said. "I thought we should be early so we can get up front."

"Like who?"

"Movie stars, maybe," Jennie answered. "It probably was just a rumor. In fact, I'm sure it was a rumor. Forget I said that."

"What are you so nervous about?" Tommy asked as they turned the last corner before Victory Square. "Which movie star was it, anyhow?"

Jennie pretended not to hear her brother. "There's Colleen and Stan." She waved at their friends.

"Did you tell Tommy about Lana Turner?" Colleen asked as soon as the two walked up.

Jennie frowned at Colleen and shook her head slightly, but it was too late.

"Lana Turner!" Tommy said. "So that's the movie star. Why didn't you just say it was her?"

"It may be just a rumor," Jennie said.

"Come on," Tommy said. "Let's get a good place to stand."

"So we can be close to the front when we win the scrap contest," Stan said.

Lana Turner forgotten, the friends staked out a spot and waited for the rally to begin. It was like the other rallies that Jennie had attended. There were speeches and music and lots of joking around by the people in charge. And always there was the plea for people to buy war bonds and stamps to help pay for the war. Jennie kept her eyes peeled, but she didn't see any sign of Lana Turner. It would almost be worth the teasing to get to see the movie star in person. She knew that lots of celebrities went all around the country appearing at rallies, but it looked like Lana Turner wasn't coming to this one.

Finally it was time to announce the winner of the scrap-collecting contest but, as usual, the emcee liked to take his time in order to build up suspense. He told stories and jokes, which sometimes made the audience groan.

"Now, the moment you've been waiting for," he said, and the crowd cheered. Jennie and the others strained forward. An assistant hurried on stage with a note that the emcee read before turning back for a whispered consultation with some other people on stage.

He motioned toward the edge of the stage before turning to the audience to announce, "We have an unexpected guest who will be coming aboard to help with the award."

There was a stir offstage. A gasp rose from the crowd as the guest walked across the stage. Jennie's eyes widened. It was Lana Turner!

The movie star moved gracefully toward the microphone, waving and smiling to the crowd, which had found its voice and now cheered loudly. She spoke briefly about the importance of buying bonds.

"And now," the emcee said, "Miss Turner will award the scrap metal-collecting prize."

Jennie and Colleen stared at each other for a moment. Would they get the prize from the hands of a famous movie star? Jennie wiped her sweaty hands on her pants just in case.

The same assistant hurried across the stage to hand the emcee a note. Again, he read it and paused for a conference before turning back to his microphone. "We have another entry in the contest that we want to show you. I think she'll be coming right through there." The emcee pointed to the back of the crowd. Sure enough, a flurry of movement began at the edge of the square.

Everyone shuffled and leaned and craned their necks to get a better look. Jennie and Colleen climbed up on a nearby bench.

"What do you see?" Tommy demanded.

"It looks like a team of horses pulling something," Colleen reported.

"What is it?" Jennie asked.

About that time the crowd parted to let the horses through. A girl about Jennie's age walked alongside an older man. Jennie couldn't see what the horses pulled but could hear scraping and crunching as it moved along the street. Then the crowd moved once more, allowing a clear view. "Why, it's a steamroller. At least it's the roller off a steamroller. It's huge."

"And made of metal, no doubt," Tommy said.

"Solid iron," Colleen said with a knowing nod.

Jennie sighed and jumped down from the bench. Colleen followed. The crowd laughed and cheered at the sight of a big iron roller being towed in by horses.

"It'll weigh a ton," Tommy said.

"More than that," Jennie said.

"More than our car?" Stan asked as he looked from Jennie to Colleen to Tommy.

"Lots more." Colleen grinned at Tommy. "No Lana Turner handshake for us."

"We didn't win the contest," Tommy said, "but we did get a lot of scrap metal for the war effort."

"Winning the war is the only contest that matters," Jennie said. The others nodded, and they all pushed through the crowd to see the lucky person who would get the award from Lana Turner.

If you enjoyed

Jennie's War

be sure to read other

SISTERS IN TIME

books from BARBOUR PUBLISHING

- Perfect for Girls Ages Eight to Twelve

- History and Faith in Intriguing Stories

- Lead Character Overcomes Personal Challenge

- Covers Seventeenth to Twentieth Centuries

- Collectible Series of Titles

6" x 8 ¼" / Paperback / 144 pages / $4.97

AVAILABLE WHEREVER CHRISTIAN BOOKS ARE SOLD